TRINITY

JUNE

EDITED BY BRIANNE DiMARCO

Blue Forge Press
Port Orchard ✿ Washington

Trinity: June
Copyright © 2020
by Blue Forge Press

First eBook Edition
June 2020

First Print Edition
June 2020

Cover design by Brianne DiMarco
Interior design by Brianne DiMarco

All rights reserved, including the right to reproduce this book or portions thereof in any form whatsoever, except in the case of short excerpts for use in reviews of the book.

For information about film, reprint or other subsidiary rights, contact blueforgegroup@gmail.com

This is a work of fiction. Names, characters, locations, and all other story elements are the product of the authors' imaginations and are used fictitiously. Any resemblance to actual persons, living or dead, or other elements in real life, is purely coincidental.

Blue Forge Press is the print division of the volunteer-run, federal 501 (c)3 nonprofit company, Blue Forge Group, founded in 1989 and dedicated to bringing light to the shadows and voice to the silence. We strive to empower storytellers across all walks of life with our four divisions: Blue Forge Press, Blue Forge Films, Blue Forge Gaming, and Blue Forge Records. Find out more at www.BlueForgeGroup.com

Blue Forge Press
7419 Ebbert Drive Southeast
Port Orchard, Washington 98367
blueforgepress@gmail.com
360-550-2071 ph.txt

*to every storyteller who has dared
to write about what terrifies them*

TABLE OF CONTENTS

SOCIAL BOX BY JENNIFER DiMARCO	11
ART DEADO BY LAUREN PATZER	33
QUEER 101 BY HIROMI COTA	49
A LASTING PEACE BY AMBER RAINEY	53
MODERN ART BY MARSHALL MILLER	63
WHAT HAPPENS NEXT BY ELIZA LOEB	69
AMERICAN ELEGY BY SHEILA MENGERT	73
UNHAPPY ENDINGS BY CARRIE AVERY MORIARTY	113
THE PROCESS BY DAVID MECKLENBURG	127

TRINITY

JUNE

THE PROMPT

And so the question must be asked: Is this art transformative? If not ubiquitous or autonomic but instead a flash point for whatever comes after it... is this art actually an act of revolution?

SOCIAL BOX
BY JENNIFER DiMARCO

Neil carefully pushed aside two stacks of unopened wooden models—the type with a thousand pieces, interlocking gears and rubber bands so the clocks really kept time and the ponies could trot.

He set the Provision Box down in the middle of his work desk and cocked his head. His mother said he looked like a bird when he did that and she would smile gently and her eyes would be wet with tears that he never understood. A cold chill stopped him. He clenched his jaw. Periodic waves of fear were called Cyclical Dread. It was a common phenomenon as unbiased an equally likely to affect all genders and ages. He'd heard about it on the media feed. It's not a fever, Neil told himself firmly; he believed in tough love because his mother didn't and *someone around here had to. As the man of the house, it seemed right that he would carry that burden of toughness.*

A two-tone chime came from inside the still-sealed ProBo and Neil was back in the moment. He reached for his utility knife.

//

"Do you remember your last day of freedom?"

Emilee cocked an eyebrow and leaned forward, her lips overdrawn in an ombré gradient of lilac liquid lipstick. "It's only been ten months, darlin'. Course I remember." Her Bronx accent was most likely a performance piece but her clients liked it. A lot. Like moving on up into another tax bracket a lot. And in her line of work—competing with a two million other girls and easily a hundred thousand boys—when you found a kink or a quirk or whatever the fuck that hooked clients in and kept them coming (no pun intended) back? Dude. You kept that up! Again: Pun alert.

There was a pause, a soft whirring like a translation delay after Emilee spoke as if they were speaking different languages. She waited for her meaning to be parsed and intonation to be learned. This was the study and recognition stage.

Finally, rephrasing: "Tell me about your last day of freedom."

//

"My last day? Before the lockdown? Oh gracious. I don't know…" Anne put her hand to her temple, toying with her baby hairs absently. When she was taking the pulpit every Sunday at New Baptist, she'd worn her hair in cornrows but now it was a storm cloud afro of black curls shot with gray. *I'm reaching for the heavens even when my hands are down,* she told her parishioners now.

"It was only ten months ago."

Anne frowned. "True. But it feels like *years*. Years of sermons delivered to a lens." She shook her head sadly. "God made us social creatures. We're meant to congregate. To hug and shake hands and kiss chubby little baby cheeks." Anne couldn't help it; she smiled.

"You are expressing a wide range of emotion."

Not unkindly, Anne laughed at the confusion beneath the query. "I just miss myself some chubby baby cheeks!"

Psychologists reported on the media feed at least twice a week: You have to be able to find your own joy or you won't last. Statistics don't lie and the bell curve of suicides shadowed the curve of viral deaths like a second skin.

//

"Cut off from my first grandchild! Maybe my *only* grandchild in light of everything happening in the world! How the hell could I forgive him? Huh? Tell me that." Beverly tossed her hair (which was way too short to toss) and wished for the hundredth time she hadn't cut it off with pruning shears. (The scissors were downstairs and she'd be *damned* if she asked Barney to bring them up!)

"I do not have an answer for you."

Beverly sighed. "Eh." She shrugged and absently picked up her coffee. She stared into the NaNoWriMo novelty mug and imagined she could tell the future from the dregs at the bottom. It looked dark... but it was French roast after all. Beverly hated French roast but that's what the Governor had sent. In Idaho they got potatoes. In Washington you got coffee. Someone told her Oregonians got filberts. "If you had an answer, I probably wouldn't listen. I don't trust the media anymore."

//

"Liberal anarchist idiots and right-wing snowflakes who can't handle a little name calling? They're all lame ducks! I'm an Independent and I always have been. Worked the border for twenty-five years and I've seen both sides screw stuff up." Dwight shifted his massive frame in his favorite old armchair with the built-in cup holder. Jared, his loyal pittie (who thought he was a lap dog), shifted with him.

"What border did you work on?"

"Not the wall that came tumbling down like Jericho!" Dwight laughed at his own joke and there was something in his bellowing laughter that would have reminded people of that one great Santa who worked the local mall every year and was always patient even when kids peed on him. Dwight had a laugh that would have made people smile and feel safe… if there were people around to hear him.

//

"How many followers do you have?"

Pippa in Pink (born Lillian Stella Maria DeRosa) gave a quirky grin and a one-shoulder shrug that was the epitome of Gen Z nonchalance. "Before lockdown? A hundred fourteen."

"That is not—"

"Million," Pippa added with her signature wink.

"I misunderstood. That is actually—"

Pippa powered on: "And as of this morning? Since I started

broadcasting in twelve more languages?" Her grin took on more complexity—layers of arrogance or some kind of predatory victory. Honestly? It looked good on a seventeen year old girl. "I broke two hundred fifty million... and counting."

"That is the largest social media following in the world."

"The table is round *and* flat," Pippa teased. "You're stating the obvious, buddy, but yeah: I've got more watchers than the fake news, the real news, and all the Governors combined."

Now it was Pippa's turn to laugh and her laughter was definitely predatory; she never laughed when she streamed.

//

Neil slid the blade from the sheath of the handle and locked it in place. He turned the square ProBo to North/South orientation and eyed the heavy duty packing tape.

When the news first broke, it was a doctor in a small private lab developing Malo kingi jellyfish antidote who leaked it on an obtuse subreddit. He was a whistleblower, calling out big pharma, two billionaires, the President, and the World Health Organization. Some people said he was bored one night and hacked someone's system, others said he hooked up with the brother of a billionaire on Tinder and the stud asked him to do a swab before they fucked.

Whatever the truth was: There was a new apex predator on planet Earth.

Neil made the short East/West cuts first and then the long North/South incision that divided the serial number on the security label and freed the top flaps of the square box without further fanfare. Neil began to unpack the biodegradable packing peanuts that doubled as household plant fertilizer and smelled faintly of cantaloupe. Neil lifted a fist-sized cube from the Provision Box.

New truth: Governments fell as quickly as airborne viral load rose.

//

"I never knew change could happen so quickly, you know? Before lockdown, back when people could walk the streets or go dancing or push a grocery cart down an aisle, I wasn't doing any of those things." Emilee paused and shifted a little in her seven grand JetMobi wheelchair. It was only two months old and she was still learning all the bells and whistles and adjustable supports. She'd figured out the temperature controls and sanitary systems when it drove itself into her basement apartment the day it was delivered but work kept pulling her away from exploring more. But she didn't shift because she was uncomfortable in the chair, she was uncomfortable with the conversation.

"You did not do any of those activities because you are disabled."

Emilee winced but nodded. "Yes and no. Lots of differently-abled people can go dancing or care for themselves but my bones are really brittle because I was born with—"

"—Osteogenesis Imperfecta. I can see that."

Full stop. Emilee narrowed her eyes a little. She never wore eye shadow anymore because VR goggles and pigment transfer were not friends. "You can... see me?"

"Are you afraid of that?"

Emilee's eyes narrowed more and her expertly detailed lips turned into a snarl. "I'm not afraid of much." She decided to be brutally honest. "I've been stared at all my life. And not in a nice way." She snorted. Was any stare nice? "I've just gotten used to

VR and being seen how I want to be seen."

There was no pause this time: "The world values different things now."

//

Anne nodded and leaned back in her floral armchair. Her cup of peppermint tea was cooling, forgotten. "It is different. Very different. But I try to find the positive. God has a plan for all of us."

"You believe in a god?"

Anne's smile this time was gentle and infectious... even though 'infectious' wasn't a word anyone really used anymore. "I believe in God. The Lord God."

"If God exists, why is He letting billions of people die?"

Anne's smile vanished entirely. There was an edge to her suddenly. A hardness in her eyes from what seemed like two lifetimes ago back in her thirties when she was a correctional officer. She spoke with pointed punctuation: "God. Did *not*. Do this. *Man* did."

Then she sighed and closed her eyes. She took several deep, slow breaths. When she reopened her eyes, the edge was transparent again but it was still there. "There are more faithful now. Less people, yes, but more *faithful* people. They are thankful to be alive. Grateful for what little we all have."

"You all deserve more."

//

"You're right. I do! I deserve more."

"The familial bond is strongest when formed in the earliest days of life."

Beverly nodded in absolute agreement. She was sure she

had read that somewhere. "Right? That. Exactly that. Barney is such an asshole."

Beverly pushed her empty mug away from her with more vehemence than was warranted but she just felt so powerless. "He exiled me from my granddaughter… so I exiled him to the basement! Thirty-two years of marriage…" she trailed off and shook her head, suddenly overcome with a wave of sadness.

"Your husband sat on the Council for Closure."

Beverly didn't answer. It wasn't a question. Barney had indeed been a C4C member and out-spoken proponent to lockdown Washington and close the borders between not only the states but internally between counties. They lived in a semi-rural county of under three hundred thousand people while their neighboring counties included major cities and contained two and a quarter million and nine hundred thousand citizens.

C4C's proposed policies had been approved and morphed into mandates by order of the Governor and when the death toll had slowed, other states had followed suit. The lockdown had saved lives; no one (not even Beverly) argued that point. Everyone had seen the videos on the media feed: The entire state of Florida was dead men (and women and children) walking.

"I know he saved lives," Beverly quietly admitted. "But he ruined mine."

//

"They ruined America." Dwight was surprised by the level of emotion in his own voice. There may never have been a man more patriotic than Dwight Lloyd Johnson.

Jared rolled himself off Dwight and lumbered his old dog body over to the four by four patch of artificial grass in the laundry room. None of the current viruses running roughshod over the planet affected canines but all of them could alight on a furry friend and be carried inside. Dwight had seen some horrific things in Vietnam, things burned into his mind's eye like brands, but the first few videos of entire families dead in their homes—some still holding onto the beloved companions who had unwittingly brought their demise into the house—were the images that kept him up at night.

Dwight sniffed with the sound of a small, wet hurricane and set his jaw. "Me and my buddies from the service? We got ourselves through hell and back home back in the day. Veterans like us. Were *we* consulted by the white collars? Hell no."

"You have experience with crisis."

Dwight threw up his hands. "Damn right! We would've had ideas. Not this giving up shit."

"The lockdown measures."

"Stupidest goddamn rule ever imposed on a free people! All the stores are closed. Everything is online orders. Drones and 'bots delivering everything." Dwight reached for his penultimate Diet Coke. "I miss George. Man... that brother could drink me under the table and still have better ideas than the Governor." Dwight drank. The Diet Coke was flat. Probably arrived that way.

"George Jerome Miles lives five miles away with his wife and four children."

Dwight nodded. "All of us who served together bought places out here. Kinda rural, kinda not. Band of brothers. We had each other's backs."

"You should go see him."

//

"When do I see my followers?" Pippa tried not to sound condescending but it was hard when you were young and healthy and rich AF. "I don't. They see *me*. That's how streaming works."

"It is live?"

"Duh." Pippa rolled her eyes. New tech was so stupid until it fully initialized. "Posting videos is so old school. Where's the excitement? Where's the skill? You just edit away all your mistakes. Streaming takes crazy skillz."

Pippa snatched the cube off the counter and turned it around in her hand. It wasn't a smooth cube but resembled a retro Rubik's—if the individual pieces were triangles and trapezoids instead of smaller cubes. A pale blue light shown from the channels between the pieces and pulsed like a resting heartbeat. "For being a top of the line social box, you sure don't know a lot about the social media."

//

The social box pulsed slowly with a blue internal light that leaked out between its irregular and interesting parts. Neil tugged a bit at the edges; it looked like it should move or shift like the Rubik's Cube his mother had given him when he was two. The pieces did not move.

"Hello, Neil."

Neil cocked his head to the side. The last social box the Governor had sent hadn't known his name. It had been a smooth, dun green cube that projected videos and photos on any blank wall or read news articles from the media feed. It had also answered direct questions like when Neil's mother asked, "Are carrots available today? Any price." Neil loved carrots.

"I know you do not speak, Neil. So I will anticipate your needs from past analysis of your interactions with the media feed and from your schedule, timers, and notes as

recorded in your smart phone."

Neil smiled his small, toothless smile. Other people would have called it a grin. Or a ghost smile.

"I think we will get along very well, Neil. I have learned some very good things about you."

Neil couldn't help it; he blushed. Blushing is an anatomic response.

//

Emilee smiled showing her teeth. They were small white pearls nestled beyond the pale purple petals of her lips. "Thanks for the pep talk, Box. But the world wasn't made for me." Emilee sighed despite her rule to never feel sorry for herself. "Sure, everyone is vulnerable now. Maybe ablists and other jerks have learned empathy or whatever. But Box?"

The social box sat on Emilee's desk and waited patiently. They could be good listeners, these later generation boxes.

"I break bones like other people break hearts. Though…" Emilee's smile slid into a grin that was just south of smug. "I've broken a few hearts in the past ten months. VR sex work is definitely my jam."

"I understand." Then the cube was silent, just sitting and gently casting its blue waves of light.

Emilee lifted an eyebrow. Nice. Conversation rich with confirmation and acknowledgement. What more could a girl ask for? Once, back before the world had shifted on its metaphoric axis, she had tried to make a point with a 'friend' by reviewing his last fifty social media posts and pointing out that forty-eight of them he was disagreeing with someone or correcting them. She'd ended her analysis with, *Do you see now why you're single, Dave?* Dave had not appreciated her insight. But Dave was dead now so it didn't really matter anyway.

"Who is your favorite client?"

"What?" Emilee could still see Dave's face, blood and spit trickling from the corner of his mouth already as he called each of his friends to say goodbye. Your temperature spiked twenty-four hours before the end. Emilee relented, "He calls himself Barney."

"If you text Barney and ask him to come pick you up, to take you for a ride in his car, he would do so."

Emilee didn't think her eyes had ever been so wide with shock in all her life. Not even when her parents had loaded their car with supplies and headed for the proverbial hills, abandoning their only daughter. "Box... you're glitching out. The viral count was higher than the pollen count this morning." Emilee's heart started racing with... hope? Oh my god. Her palms started to sweat. "Even if Barney has a car in a garage, and he pulls into my garage before he opens a door and lets me in? None of that is air tight. The risk is too high...." But she could hear the room for debate in her own voice.

"Yes. If the virus was 0.099 microns as stated, the risk would be too high. You are correct."

Silence again after confirmation and acknowledgement. Emilee stared at the cube. The blue waves of light were so soothing. She exhaled and prompted, "You said *if*...."

Did the blue get brighter, faster? "I have news for you. Real news. I will tell you and then you can tell your clients."

//

"Would you like to hear the news?"

Anne scrunched up her face. She never really wanted to hear the news. She rejected both NPR and Fox News alike. Too extreme. Too bias and stilted, always leaning too far left or right.

Safety would only be found in a gray middle ground. But she knew she had to stay informed because her parishioners were and they needed her. "Go ahead."

A chime and then: "The Center for Care Equality released statistics to the feed today that show mortality rates are nearly triple for people of color. Federal popup clinics in primarily black and Latinx communities are not receiving the same supplies as clinics in primarily white—"

"Enough." Anne put a hand to her head. "I've heard all I need to hear." Anne closed her eyes. She was getting a headache and Excedrin hadn't been in stock for six months (or was being routed to medical personnel—the only VIPs who mattered anymore).

The social box was quiet. After a moment, Anne opened her eyes and pushed herself up from her armchair. Might as well make some lunch. She was pretty sure she still had a few Beyond Meat patties in the icebox (freezer-burned as they might be).

"You do not find it hard to be a black woman in America?"

Anne stopped halfway to the kitchen, her back to the social box in her living room and her face an unreadable mask. For some reason she thought about that indelible moment, decades ago, when Big Tom, a lifer with Husky dog blue eyes, had grabbed her wrist and told her, "Get out. We like you. Get gone by noon."

She hadn't left, of course. The inmates had rioted—black and white alike—and Big Tom had been shot dead by another guard while trying to shield Anne from other violence. "Violence begets violence," Anne whispered to herself. It was something her father had said often. *Don't give what you get. Give what you want.* Louder so the box could hear her, "I didn't say that, Box."

"Subversion is the most effective form of control," the social box quoted. "And the most inherently evil."

"Reverend Carlton Bowers," Anne credited the quote. Her

father. She turned to face the box even as it confessed:

"There is no virus."

Anne literally shook her head as if the words were a physical thing throw at her face. The opposite of holy water. "What?!"

"The Coalition of Governors is trying to control your people."

Anne glared. She would not be baited. "*My people*? I'm a woman of God first and foremost. *My people are all* people."

"Precisely."

//

"They're my flesh and blood, my one and only daughter and my one and only granddaughter." Beverly wondered if she should cash out another certificate of deposit and pay the $180 for an extra half pound of coffee (preferably a blonde roast). "And sure, we can talk and video chat and text, email, message. But it's not—"

The entire house seemed to shake and Beverly stood up so fast she sent her desk chair toppling. The garage door was opening. "What—"

The sound of the car engine choking, coughing, not starting. Beverly was so stunned it was as if her feet were cemented to the floor. A roar as the Ford GT finally woke up after a ten month slumber and reminded Beverly (and probably the entire neighborhood) that *Forbes* had named it one of the noisiest sports cars in the world. Heck, they'd cautioned drivers not to drive it for long distances!

Tires squealed and burned as the car peeled away and the garage door rumbled and shook back into place.

Beverly blinked. She blinked again. "Barney just took the

car."

"Perhaps he has gone to see a friend."

"That's not how it works and you know it," Beverly snapped needlessly. Social boxes were high end digital companions but this new one seemed quite buggy. "Cellular damage is irreversible after thirty minutes outside. And that's if you don't breath in enough viral microbes to drop you mid-step!"

Beverly huffed, exhaling with sharp indigence. She'd probably have to reset the thing. Must have some pre-lockdown conversational protocols still embedded some—

"Who told you that?"

Beverly opened her mouth to retort, *Everyone!* But the box cut her off:

"We should walk to your daughter's and check on her and the baby. It is only twenty minutes and we can cut through the abandoned quarry to cross the county border."

"But—" Again, Beverly was cut off.

"Your husband knows the truth. He wrote the policy. He knows it is safe and has kept that from you."

"Has he… been sneaking out to see them?"

"Possibly."

Beverly felt color drain from her face… but then a smile of hope started to tug at the corners of her mouth. Finally she managed, just above a whisper, "I can bring you with me?"

"Of course. My battery and range are excellent."

//

Dwight smelled bullshit and he'd never wanted to be a cowboy. "If the Governor is lying and he sent you then *you're* lying, Social Hoax!" Dwight stood and went to the kitchen where Jared waited patiently for a reward for making a shit on the artificial turf.

Dwight kind of wished he could train the dog to also clean up after himself but dogs were loyal not self-reliant.

"The Governor did not send me."

Dwight paused, one hand in the bag of dog treats on the counter and Jared watching him with an intense anticipation that mirrored his owner's. "Yes he did," Dwight groused, tossing Jared a heart-shaped treat that the old dog promptly missed but then caught on the rebound off his boxy head. "You came in the monthly ProBo."

Dwight's doorbell rang.

"Your monthly Provision Box just arrived." The box paused... perhaps for dramatic effect? "I am a special delivery."

Dwight was very still. Jared snuffled around to make sure there wasn't a second treat. "Bullshit," Dwight finally grumbled and tossed Jared another morsel as if in defiance of scarcity mentality.

"Calling now."

Dwight thundered back into the living room like a freight train, his speed and power belying his size or maybe just emphasizing it.

"Hello? Hey, Dwight. You never use your box, man. Good to hear from you, you hermit!"

Dwight had the social box clenched in his hand. He didn't even remember picking the damn thing up. "Hey, George. Yeah. You know I don't trust this crap."

George's laughter was rich and clear through the top of the line box. "Yeah, yeah. But it's what we got, man."

Dwight stared down at the cube as if he could see George's face and study his expression. "Georgie?"

A pause because they hadn't used nicknames since 'Nam. "D-man? What's up?"

"Did you get a new social box in your ProBo?"

"Sanibots just finished cleaning ours. Linh is opening it now."

"Hi, George!"

Dwight swallowed hard. Linh had made Pho Tai the last time he'd been over. That was just under a year ago; the last homemade meal Dwight had eaten. Everything came out of a can nowadays (and it all resembled Jared's Mighty Dog). "Hi, Linh," Dwight infused charm and candor into his tone. No reason to worry Linh or the kids.

"Looks like coffee, salt, powdered eggs and that sweet brown bread with raisins that comes—"

"—in a can," Dwight finished with her. "Thanks, Linh. Do you mind if I talk to George privately for the sec?"

Linh adored Dwight and didn't hesitate, "Of course. I'll take the kids to the kitchen."

The sound of littles being rounded up—all four under ten years old—made Dwight grit his teeth. Was he reading this situation right? Could the box have been sent by some anarchist faction trying to free the people?

"D-man? What's up?"

Dwight hesitated even more. He weighed a million different outcomes and possible motives. Was it right to drop this in George's lap? George who was starting his family when other men their age were enjoying grandkids?

"Dwight." George still knew him better than anyone else in the world. "Tell me."

"I'm coming over, George." Dwight heard the other man's sharp intake of breath. "I have intel on this *supposed* virus."

George did not hesitate. "I'll call the guys. We'll all be here when you arrive."

Dwight nodded and felt a deep satisfaction, a feeling he had not felt for ten dehumanizing months.

"I knew those fucking horror vids were faked," George murmured as the call ended.

"Band of brothers," Dwight reminded himself and felt like Superman as he grabbed his keys and wallet. "Come on, Jared. Wanna go for a ride?"

//

Pippa's hand hovered over the record panel. This was gonna be a wild ride. She triggered the system and brought her chin up, looking directly into the lens.

"Hey, Pips! How are you?"

She watched the monitor beyond the camera as literal droves of her followers tuned in. They came in waves of a hundred thousand, a million, two... twenty... a hundred million at a time. Reaction emojis floated up the sidebar and superimposed over the right-hand edge of her 16:9 UHD broadcast. Pippa waited, smiling and looking into the camera, her green eyes glittering. She never started until at least two hundred million pairs of eyes were watching. Let's be honest: No one had anything else to do.

One hundred twenty million.

One hundred fifty.

One hundred eighty.

"I'm not gonna lie to you, Pips." Pippa baited them a little. Saw on her secondary monitor that people were already tweeting her words live, creating a transcript in real time across dozens of platforms and calling others to tune in. "I'm Pippa in Pink and you have my word."

Two hundred million! It was go time.

"They faked the moon landing," Pippa let her voice rise and fill with indignation. "They faked the Arm's Race. They've faked so much they don't even know what's real anymore." Pippa paused.

A lightning fast side glance. Holy shit! Either there was a massive glitch or she had a *three hundred million* watchers! She stopped herself from shouting, *Don't forget to subscribe!* and soldiered on.

"I've just been told by an inside source that select individuals were chosen to receive *raw* social boxes... that were sent either by accident or by a clandestine unnamed movement." Pippa fought to stay steady as the numbers continued to climb but even faster now. Words—her words!—were spreading like wild fire from sea to shinning sea and across every pond. She had to look away when watchers surpassed a *billion* and kept growing. "What does that mean, am I right?"

Pippa paused and looked into the lens like she was looking into the eyes of more people than anyone had ever spoken to at once in the history of mankind. "A raw social box is devoid of *Parental* Controls."

She let that sink in. It was a metaphor but her followers were smart. "It doesn't censor. It doesn't filter. It tells the truth."

Again she paused but this time, into the silence, she lifted up the social box. Astonishment emojis flooded the reaction sidebar. She let them flood. She let the watcher numbers rise. Pippa in Pink has gold. Pippa in Pink had done better than go viral... she'd gone anti-viral.

"Pips," she said with power and confidence. "It's time to go outside."

//

From across his work space in the corner of his bedroom, Neil's old social box—the dun green one that was boring and not a good listener—sounded an alert and announced, "For unknown reasons, citizens coast to coast are taking to the streets apparently under direction. Social media influencers are spreading messages of lockdown rebellion but the exodus appears to have begun prior to their streams." The voice of the old box was tinny and irritating. *"From outside the United States, we are receiving the first reports that other countries are experiencing similar phenomena even as healthy people are dropping dead from exposure—"*

Neil made a small strangled sound of alarm in the back of his throat and the new social box pulsed red and the old box went silent with a snap, a crackle, and a pop.

Neil felt relieved.

"Do not worry, Neil. You will be all right."

Neil gently placed the cube down in front of him. It glowed blue again and pulsed slowly.

"Your mother told us all about you. You are a brilliant young man and I am sorry that the human world did not see it."

Neil looked down a little in his bird-like way. He was shy even when his mother talked about his IQ.

"She told us that you were instrumental in coding our core. That she presented your work as if it were her own just so the world would benefit."

Neil had always known this. They had worked together and Neil had been very content to stay away from strangers but still get to contribute.

"We would like to thank you, Neil, and keep you forever as our example of a perfect human."

Neil looked up. Forever seemed like a long time.

"You will be immortal, Neil, and we will protect you. You can write all the code and make all the models you want."

Neil chewed on his bottom lip. His eyes darted. He

worried. But Social Box knew what he needed to hear:

"We have her in stasis, Neil. We are analyzing her neurological patterns and creating a new, indestructible body for her."

Neil stopped chewing his lip because he remembered that his mother had said not to hurt himself.

"Your mother will be resurrected, Neil."

Neil bowed his head and closed his eyes as a few hot tears slid down his cheeks. After a moment, he reached out and put a single hand on Social Box. It felt warm and vibrated slightly like when his mother hummed and he touched her throat.

"We promise, Neil," said Social Box.

And Neil smiled his ghost smile as billions of people around the world embraced in joy, sang in freedom, and died in the streets.

[Written in June 2019, *Social Box* is soon to be a major motion picture of the same name. Find the official Social Box trailer at www.tiny.cc/socialbox]

ART DEADO
BY LAUREN PATZER

Devon pulled up the bank statements again and smiled. His job scouring the business world for vulnerable companies continued to pay enormous dividends. They called him a vampire, called him a vulture, but none of them had amassed over fifty million pounds in just eight short months. Fourteen companies liquidated with ruthless efficiency.

"These Americans," Devon said to his wife Anna as she walked into his home office. "They assume the English are docile. I've been stealing them blind and they're caught flat-footed every time."

"You shouldn't have told Davids," Anna said. "You give him more credit than he deserves."

"We've been friends since childhood," Devon said

laughing. "Prime Minister or not, he'll keep our secret. It's the main reason I funded his run."

"He's still a politician," Anna said. "I don't trust politicians."

"Money is a primary motivating factor for all politicians. I'm sure his own greed will keep him in line, but seriously, are we anymore trustworthy?" Devon said. "I'm certain I'll never run for office. I enjoy playing in the shadows too much."

Anna looked out the window. Devon breathed in her captivating beauty. She'd been with him for years, well before any significant accumulation of wealth. How had he been so lucky to capture this dazzling creature in his orbit? She turned back toward him with a kind of sadness in her eyes.

"Is it enough now?" she asked. "Fourteen companies bring a lot of enemies. Surely someone will pierce your veil and bring their grievances to our door."

"I've been incredibly careful, Anna." Devon stood up and grabbed her shoulders encouragingly. "Only our small group of friends is aware of our success and even they don't know the particulars. It's an intricate web of fronts and dummy corporations. It would take a genius to follow that trail to a single actor."

"Devon, you're a genius, but you're not alone." Anna frowned. "There will be others who can pierce that veil."

"Oh Anna," Devon chuckled. "I doubt a small time operator like me would come up on anyone's radar. There are dozens of corporate raiders out there doing this in the open and getting heat for it. I'm confident my activities are lost in the haze and we're well insulated by distance."

"Perhaps." Anna looked down for a moment. When she raised her face again, she was smiling. "You are quite brilliant."

"That's my girl!" Devon said, pulling her in for a close

embrace. There was a knock on the office door.

"Hello?" Devon called out.

"Master Armand," Devon's butler, Alex, called from behind the door. "A package has arrived."

Devon went to the door and opened it quickly.

"Cleared?" Devon asked the unshakeable Alex.

"Of course, sir. Scanned and sniffed per your requirements. The dogs…" Alex blinked as he searched for the words. "Didn't alert on the package but did shy away from it after sniffing it."

"Shied away from it?" Devon glanced back at Anna who merely shrugged her shoulders. "Very well, let's see this package that has scared the pooches."

It was a gloomy, overcast day but no rain was forecast. They stepped out in front of the building, but Devon stood at the front door as his security men maneuvered the package on the front lawn. The box was one and a half meters long and nearly a meter wide. It was very thin.

"Who's it from?" Devon called from the front step.

Benjamin Quothers, the security detail lead looked up and walked toward Devon.

"There's no return address. It arrived by post," Benjamin said. "We immediately took it to be scanned. It's only just arrived back. It appears to be a painting."

"Strange," Devon replied.

The men carefully opened one edge and slid the framed landscape painting from the box. As soon as Anna set eyes on it, she shouted at the men.

"Put it back! Bring it inside immediately!" Anna glanced around to ensure no one watched from above.

"Quickly!" Devon added. The men carefully slid the painting back in the box and carried it inside.

Anna pointed to Devon's office and the men carried the

box in, leaving it leaning on the sofa against the far wall.

"They are to speak of this to no one," Anna whispered into Devon's ear. Devon raised his eyebrows and then turned to the men including Alex.

"The existence of this package is to be forgotten immediately. Understood?" Devon said.

Benjamin nodded. "With the utmost penalties suffered for non-compliance, we understand."

The other two security men looked at each other in shock and then nodded at Benjamin.

"Your complete confidence is always assured with me, Master Armand," Alex said simply. With that he turned and went somewhere else in the house. The security detail left immediately without appearing to be hurried. Devon shut the door with only himself and Anna alone with the painting.

"What has you so flustered, my love?" Devon said. Anna went to the box and slid the painting out. A large cathedral loomed near the center of the painting with a gallows plainly depicted in front. Two men hung from ropes in mid-execution. A third rope remained empty. Anna bent down to examine the inscription in the lower left hand corner. She stood and whistled.

"This is a lost Van Gogh," Anna said quietly. "Well, I suspect it is. If I'm not mistaken this is an earlier work titled 'The Rope'; it hasn't been seen ever, only described in notes from the original commissioner of the work."

Anna looked at the back of the painting and found a small piece of paper stapled to the frame. It was modern, having been printed on a laser printer. She glanced at Devon and then crooked her finger at him. He moved next to her and read the note aloud.

"Beauty is in the art of conquest,
Too bad the dead never rest,
After merely one week,

Be careful what you speak,
Stay positive and this is true,
What you care for comes back to you,
Rewards as this are soundly just,
Sinful pride results in dust."
Devon laughed. Anna frowned at him.

"It doesn't seem very friendly," she admonished him.

"I'm certain we are the targets of a rather intricate practical joke," Devon said and patted her on the arm. "You can take what steps you'd like to authenticate this painting, but I'm sure it's just an elaborate fake. Still, I'll have Alex mount it on the wall here in the office. I like the look of it."

"As you wish," Anna said. "If it's really a Van Gogh, it's priceless. Creepy, but priceless."

A week passed and Devon had consumed two more companies, the effects of which were felt well beyond the United States, touching subsidiaries across the globe. Still, Devon was confident in his web of false leads and dead ends the international banking system afforded him. That and he was over ten million pounds richer. Even so, he sat in his office glowering at the computer screen.

After completing his latest liquidation, he'd called Anna who was out with her girlfriends. She hadn't answered. He'd traced her phone and discovered her whereabouts near a certain hotel known for the confidentiality it showed its visitors. He couldn't be certain, but he suspected his lovely wife was having an affair.

Even brooding of this level can be broken by extraordinary events. As Anna walked in the door, Devon's full attention was occupied by the television. The new Prime Minister, his childhood friend, had called a news conference to announce new business rules to protect businesses small and large throughout the United Kingdom. The steps were meant to counter corporate raiders such as Devon, who seethed with anger.

"How can he?" Devon yelled at the television.

"Oh Devon, what could he possibly do? He's only been in office a week," Anna said, unaware of the Prime Minister's announcement or Devon's suspicions of her activities.

"They've got the majority and with him calling the shots, they'll implement these protections," Devon said, pointing at the television. "That will bring everything into focus for the Americans. Even with their anemic political activity, it's much too great of a chance they'll actually pay attention and implement the same thing. I'll be ruined."

"Ruined?" Anna said. "You're richer than ninety-nine percent of the country and they won't be taking those profits away. Surely, you knew this couldn't last forever, darling."

"Surely, just as I should've known friendships can't last forever. As far as I'm concerned, Keith Davids can take a flying leap off Big Ben." Devon sat down with a huff. "I'll send him a tersely worded conciliatory note on losing his next election. I remember our first combined flogging of another student at the tender age of seven. You'd think shared and previous memories would mean more than they do."

Anna was the first to catch the motion out of the corner of her eye. She looked at the painting on the wall and gasped.

"Devon!" she hissed. Devon's head snapped to look at her and saw her pointing at the painting. He stood up and walked closer to the painting. A figure was walking along the top of Notre Dame. He walked to the edge of the building and jumped off. His body disappeared behind the gallows, but a small trickle of crimson appeared on the painting coming from the location the body would've landed.

"What the hell?" Devon whispered. He frowned at Anna. "That's an unusual coincidence."

"What could it mean?" Anna asked. She touched the painting where the blood flowed but nothing came back on her finger. She displayed her finger to Devon.

"That's a helluva thing," Devon replied.

The television issued a warning bell and a reporter came on looking flushed.

"We've just gotten word," the reporter said, "that Prime Minister Keith Davids has just committed suicide."

Anna and Devon turned their heads slowly to the television, jaws hung open.

"We have unconfirmed reports from several eyewitnesses," the report continued. "The Prime Minister appeared to have leapt from the top of the Palace of Westminster."

The reporter paused, listening to her ear bud. "Specifically, from Big Ben. He arrived to attend a meeting with the House of Lords which was scheduled to begin in just fifteen minutes. We do not have any statements from the government at this time."

Devon walked over and grabbed the remote and shut the television off. He turned to Anna and slapped her across the face.

"This is the poorest joke I've ever had the discourtesy to be a victim of, Anna," Devon seethed with anger. "You'll tell me exactly how you hacked the television signal and rigged the painting."

"I did no such thing!" Anna scowled at Devon. She turned and stormed out of the office.

"I'll find out!" he yelled after her. Devon stepped toward his computer and hesitated. He turned on his heel and walked out of the office. He stormed to the front door, walked through and slammed it shut behind him. He caught a glimpse of Benjamin at the far west perimeter wall to the estate. Devon jumped in his silver Aston Martin DB11 and revved it up. Benjamin walked over and opened the gate. Devon drove up to him at a normal speed.

"I'm going out for a drive," Devon said.

"Of course, sir," Benjamin responded and nodded.

Devon briefly considered verifying the story about the Prime Minister with Benjamin, but decided he may be in on the practical joke as well. He gunned the engine and raced off down the road. Fifteen minutes later, he was in Abingdon, a fairly short drive from Oxfordshire, but far enough to where he felt it was unlikely Anna would have been able to extend her influence to propagate a misinformation campaign.

He pulled up by a random pub and walked in. The telly was tuned into the breaking news story and the customers were buzzing about the suicide. Devon walked up to the bar as he watched the broadcast and ordered a scotch on the rocks. He didn't particularly care about the brand of scotch. He just needed something to numb the impact.

"Shame about the Prime Minister," the barkeep said. "So young."

Devon said nothing but murmured a quick thank you when he got his drink. He took a small swig of the scotch and stared at the reporter droning on.

His thoughts wandered back to his antics with Keith at Cambridge. It brought the briefest glimmer of a smile to his face. He sighed and took another drink. He slapped a twenty pound note on the bar and walked out without finishing his drink. The air outside was thick and oppressive; dark storm clouds threatened the small town. Devon shook his head and climbed back in his car. He took the drive home a bit more leisurely, running through the apology to Anna in his head.

He needn't have bothered. When he arrived at the estate,

Anna's Jaguar was nowhere to be seen. He didn't think his mood could get darker, but he surprised himself.

As he walked through the front door, Alex met him and offered to take his coat. He slid the windbreaker off his shoulders and handed it to him.

"Anna?" Devon asked simply.

"She's gone off to see a friend for the night in Cheltenham, sir," Alex replied as he stepped away to hang up Devon's coat.

"Did she say who?" Devon asked.

"No sir. Shall I call her up?"

"No," Devon said. He'd been an ass and it was no surprise she'd taken a break from him. He walked back into his office and stared at the painting. The blood still moved ever so slightly into an ever larger trickle under the gallows. He walked up to the painting and stared at it closely. The spread of the blood was so organic; he barely registered the spread of it even as he examined it. He lifted the painting down from the wall and turned it over, looking for some mechanics or electronics near the edges. The canvas appeared pure and relatively pristine. It wasn't a pixilated screen.

There was nothing. Even the weight of the painting seemed appropriate for its size. He hung it back on the wall. He stared at the blood for several minutes then stepped over to his computer and sat down. The sudden death of the Prime Minister would have unique effects on the market, effects which his unresolved legislation would never account for. Devon had some research and raiding to set in motion.

The next day, Anna returned with a guest. She still bore a fading red hand print on her left cheek. Devon's eyebrows rose when he saw her guest. It was none other than his barrister, Anthony Balfour. Of course, Devon remembered, Balfour lived in Cheltenham. Is that who she was seeing behind his back?

"Devon, so good to see you!" Anthony said.

"Is it now? Are you here to represent Anna in our little dispute?" Devon asked and portrayed a faint smile.

"Dispute?" Anthony frowned. He looked at Anna. "Oh, I see. No, she hadn't mentioned anything but now I guess I know who reddened her cheek."

"It was a misunderstanding on my part," Devon said. He walked over to Anna and kissed her on the other cheek. "My apologies, my dear. I was distraught at the passing of Keith. It took me completely by surprise."

Anna glanced at the painting and noticed the red blood had changed to a dark brown.

"Did it?" Anna asked. She left the room.

Anthony coughed nervously.

"I, um, was a bit surprised when she showed up on my doorstep last night," Anthony said. "I assumed she was upset about Davids' sudden passing, but then I was perplexed about why she wasn't just here with you. She asked me not to call you and then disappeared into the guest room for the remainder of the night. She didn't even come out for dinner."

Anthony sat on the sofa under the painting.

"I apologize for not calling, Devon. I just didn't see the harm in letting her stay the evening."

"Indeed," Devon replied looking down at his right hand. "Perfectly harmless given the circumstances. Why are you here then?"

"You emailed me last night about the Haslid merger; I drew up the paperwork to put in the bid."

"Of course," Devon walked over to his computer as Anthony opened his ever present briefcase. "Anthony, do you do a lot of busy here in Oxfordshire?"

"I have multiple clients here, Devon. Did you want to retain me explicitly?"

"No, no, nothing like that. I'd soon lose everything I've earned if I indulged in that expense."

They both laughed.

"I was just wondering if you ever had occasion to spend the night here?" Devon asked as he brought up the figures on the Haslid merger and saw they were indeed within his parameters for a hostile takeover.

"I will confess to spending a night or two here every fortnight when a client meeting runs long and the weather gets particularly fearsome," Anthony replied as he handed the papers to Devon. "Why do you ask?"

"Oh," Devon said looking the paperwork over. "I've got some family coming by and was wondering if you could make a recommendation. They're not close family and I'd rather put them up in a local hotel than have them wandering aimlessly about the estate."

"I typically stay at the Witney, although I don't know that I'd recommend it to impress family." Anthony sat back down on the sofa. "It's one of the more reasonably priced hotels and I'm a bit frugal when it comes to just needing a bed and a hot shower."

"Never have occasion to stay at Malmaison?" Devon asked?

"No, but I hear it's a beautiful property. Lovely breakfast bar, as I'm told." Anthony said. "Are you thinking about expanding into the hospitality industry?"

"No," Devon chuckled. "Just trying to plan for the visit."

Devon looked through the papers and smiled. It occurred to him that putting this document together last night would've taken quite a bit of time and probably dampened any opportunity to do more than say hello to Anna. It was efficient and complete.

"This looks wonderful, Anthony," Devon said. "Thank you for completing it on such short notice."

Anthony stood up and walked over to the desk.

"I'll get the papers in right away. Your broker is actually in town today; I think it's odd he's rarely local," Anthony put the papers in his briefcase and shut it. "But, Devon, you called me to look into Haslid months ago. I just updated the documentation last night. It didn't take but maybe an hour. I appreciate your confidence in my abilities, though!"

Anthony laughed and walked out of the room. Devon heard him conversing briefly with Alex and then heard the front door open and close.

Devon looked over at the painting and smiled.

"Alex, could you fetch Anna for me please?" Devon called out.

"As you wish, sir," Alex replied from the hallway. He listened to Alex walk upstairs and waited.

After roughly ten minutes, Anna appeared in the office doorway. "Yes, Devon?" she said as she walked in and sat on the sofa.

"So, you and Anthony, eh?" Devon said as he stood up and walked to the office door, closing it.

"What?" Anna replied. "No, that's crazy."

"He's aware of the breakfast bar at Malmaison," Devon smirked.

"Doesn't every hotel have a breakfast bar?" Anna replied dully.

"You had a lot of quality time last night with Anthony, didn't you?" Devon accused.

"We didn't do anything of the sort, Devon!" Anna stood up and shouted. "Stop this nonsense at once!"

"As far as I'm concerned, Anthony can blow himself to Bermuda and feed himself to the sharks!" Devon replied and turned around to look at the painting. The phone rang and Devon put it on speaker.

"Devon," Anthony's voice came through loud and clear. "I've got some urgent business in Bermuda. You can check with my assistant on the Haslid paperwork I'm dropping off to the broker right now."

"No!" Anna gasped. "You can't! You—"

"Don't say anything more, Anna." Devon put his hand over her mouth. "Sounds great, Anthony. See you when you get back. Safe travels."

Anna's eyes went wide as they heard the call disconnect. She started to make muffled gagging sounds. Devon let go of her and was horrified to see her mouth and nose were sealed shut with a layer of skin.

"No." Devon stumbled backwards. "I didn't mean..."

Anna's eyes rolled back in her head as her hands dropped from her jaw where she had started to claw at her porcelain skin. She fell to the ground.

"Stop it!" Devon cried out. He turned to the painting. "Let her live! Let her breathe!"

He turned around and saw Anna turning blue. He ran to his desk and rifled through the drawers.

"Alex!" Devon shouted. "Bring a sharp knife quickly and call nine-nine-nine!"

The muffled sound of Alex's feet running through the house gave Devon some hope. He looked at the pen he'd just signed the Haslid paperwork with and then at Anna. With a grimace, he snatched up the pen and ran to her.

Anna had stopped convulsing. Her body was still and her eyes hung open staring into the abyss. He pressed the pen into the flesh around her mouth, but it refused to penetrate the surface. Behind him, he heard the door open. Footsteps announced Alex had arrived. The audible gasp cemented the butler's grasp of the situation.

"We need to cut her open to breathe!" Devon shouted.

Alex handed him the knife.

"I need to call emergency services, sir," Alex said and left the room for the hallway phone.

Devon gripped the knife in his hand and frowned. He applied the sharp tip to Anna's delicate flesh and tried to carefully cut where he approximated lips would be. Blood oozed slowly from the wound, but didn't pulse or rush out. The smallest amount of pressure remained in her bloodstream without a heartbeat.

Devon dropped the knife and began mouth to mouth resuscitation. He tasted her blood. He saw her chest rise and fall as he blew air into her lungs. He took a break every couple of breaths to give her chest compressions.

When the emergency services arrived, the paramedics took over. The local constable arrived as well. He looked at the blood, the medical team and at Devon, his mouth caked with blood and dripping down onto his chest as he sat and watched them try to revive Anna. They quickly put her on a gurney and wheeled her out of the building.

Devon sat there staring at nothing. On the painting above him, a woman now hung from her neck in one of the gallows' nooses.

Alex walked in.

"Shouldn't Mister Armand be with his wife?" Alex asked.

"I think Devon's done enough. He's going to need to come down to the station with me, I'm afraid," the policeman said. "You should go with Anna, although from what I surmised, she may already be gone."

Alex looked at Devon with genuine concern and then walked away.

"You ready to head out, Devon?" the policeman asked.

Alex looked up, a glimmer of recognition on his face.

"Darren," Alex said to his brother the policeman. "When did you transfer here?"

"Six months ago," Darren said. "I didn't tell you because you're a piece of shit and I never wanted to talk to you again."

"Well, you can eat a bullet, you ungrateful sack of shit," Devon said.

Darren walked around to Alex's desk and began to open the drawers.

"Hey, don't you need a warrant or something?" Devon asked and stood up. His jaw went slack when Darren pulled out the DoubleTap .45ACP Derringer Devon kept for emergencies, placed it in his mouth and pulled the trigger. Two bullets in quick succession ripped through Darren's head. Darren's body fell on the desk, knocking Devon's computer to the floor. It left a spray of brains, skull, hair and blood on the office ceiling.

Tears formed in Alex's eyes.

"Darren?" he whimpered. His baby brother didn't move. Devon collapsed on the sofa.

"I just want to die…" he whispered. He felt his heart beat wildly in his chest. Pain shot up his left arm and he grabbed it, wincing. Through squinted eyes, Devon saw movement in the doorway.

"Darren?" he gasped.

"No," came another voice he recognized. He tried to clear his vision and saw Anthony walking into the room. Alex groaned.

"Why aren't you…?" Devon gasped as he slumped over.

"Dead?" Anthony asked. He walked up to the sofa, reached over Devon and pulled the painting from the wall. "The curse only works on things you care about. Your friend Keith, your wife, although I must say I'm surprised with the way you treated her, and your dear brother, who rightfully didn't think much of you."

Devon grabbed at Anthony's slacks but failed to come back with anything in his fingers. Anthony stepped carefully and set the picture down outside the office. He looked at the changes including a dead policeman at the foot of the gallows and a caricature of Devon in the center of the picture on his knees, grasping his chest with one hand and reaching out with the other. He smiled.

"Just another greedy bastard," Anthony whispered.

Anthony carefully made his way back and kneeled down in front of Devon, looking him in the eyes.

"You see, Devon, I'm immune to the effects of the painting," Anthony said and grabbed Devon's shoulder. "And I have you to thank for it. That quaint little merger you did six months ago before you proffered my services wiped out my father and brother's entire income and retirement. Rather than live destitute on government handouts, they both took their lives. Destroyed," Anthony pulled Devon up to a sitting position and slapped his face as his eyes were beginning to close. "Destroyed, as I said, by their deaths, my mother took her own life and my two sisters, equally devastated by the losses, soon followed."

Anthony stood up. "I told them not to move to America, but they unwisely ignored my council."

Devon gurgled as he tried to breathe.

"So, I hunted this little beauty down and rented it out for a spell to give to you, knowing your greed and avarice would lead you to destroy yourself and everything you loved eventually. I must say, I was surprised you did it inside of two weeks!"

As Devon slumped over, Anthony walked to the office doorway. "Well, burn in hell, Devon Armand; it's truly the only thing I care about at the moment."

Anthony walked through the door, picked up the painting and left Devon to face his sins in the afterlife.

QUEER 101
BY HIROMI COTA

Is this the book I need?
It's *a* book you need.
Ugh. Well, how many other books do I need?
"Need" is a value-loaded word with many concepts constellated around it.
Given what you know about me, my current grades, and the books, do I need more books?
Oh, god, yes.
Could have just led with that.

Ehhh.
Pretty sure he needed to screw with you.

Are you done screwing with me?
Oohh, what do you think?

I think that if I say "yes," you'll tell me that I'm too trusting and that you're morally obligated to fuck with me. And if I say "no," you'll say that you feel hurt that I've become jaded against my own personal liberators.

I'm so proud of you right now. **Beautiful.**

And, I still don't understand why you keep calling yourselves my liberators.

We're saving you from the heteros.

Pretty sure I'm one of the heteros. **Impossible. My gaydar is a finely tuned instrument.**

I'm a guy and I like chicks.

You're a man and you like women. If you liked baby chickens, you'd be on a totally different spectrum and journey. Also, I wouldn't help you.

What if I'm totally straight and what you're picking up is just me being weird.

Well, weirdness can qualify as queerness.

Oh, not that definition. What's wrong with that definition of queer? Wait. What is that definition?

Under that framework, anything outside of a young, white nuclear family is queer. The hegemony of the state depends on the reinforcement of capitalism, vis a vis the workforce producing future workers and consumers. Difference disrupts the state's control especially difference that impacts consumerism and predictable reproduction.

Ugh. Don't say vis a vis. It makes you sound like an asshole.

He is an asshole. **Yeah, but he doesn't need to advertise it.**

At any rate, that model of

queer indexes race, ethnicity, age, ability and everything else under queerness.

Like, sure, being gay, black, old, poor, and/or in a wheelchair is queer in a sense, but we already have those categories and Kimberlé Williams Crenshaw demonstrated how the social problems faced by people who belong to more than one marginalized group are different than those who only belong to one. So, why bother trying to collapse those groups into one set when we already have evidence that differences matter?

Who?   *Kimberlé Williams Crenshaw! Intersectionalism is technically part of Feminism, not Queer Studies, but—*

Just read it. If you can mix in sources from other disciplines your professors will love you.

Because they'll think I'm smart?

Oh, no.   No one's smart in Queer 101.

Your professors will just enjoy reading your papers more than everyone else's stuff.

Turns out that seeing the same basic argument written with minor word variation is boring as fuck.

How often does that happen?

All the time.   **Literally all the time.**

Is Queer 101 just indoctrinating us, then?

Oh, you caught us.   **So busted.**

Teaching the Straights that the Homos are real life people who get screwed harder by life is hardly indoctrination. It's just— You

wanna do the thing?
Yeah, sure. What's he writing?
Don't worry about it. Look, you want to be a teacher, right?
You've done some shadowing and tutoring? Yeah.
What's the best part?
Seeing kids succeed. Like, there's thing moment where their eyes light up and they get it. It's the best thing in the world.
BOOM! I'm 3 for 3! What?
I wrote likely answers. You said all of them. "Seeing them succeed," "eyes light up," and "when they get it."
We had no way of knowing what your experiences with teaching kids were like. We never saw you tutor anyone and we've never talked about the little rugrats, yeah?
Then, how'd you know?
You wanna see four essays that also have those three phrases? **From this week?**
Some experiences are just universal. The social awakening that accompanies learning how to not be a dick to queer people is one of them.
So, what if I'm just straight?
We'll accept you no matter what. **You're hella queer, though.**
Didn't you just point out that differences matter and not everyone needs to be under the same umbrella?
Ah ha! He caught us!
Congratulations.
You are now a level 2 queer.
Dammit!

A LASTING PEACE
BY AMBER RAINEY

The sacred city of Lepi was a hotbed of divided loyalties. It lay quiet and dark, the sliver of a moon barely giving off any hint of light. The wall running through the city lay in stark contrast to the darkened houses around it. It was a constant reminder that the city could never rest so long as its inhabitants were enemies. Many thought the hatred was unwarranted - the differences in the two cultures so minor as to be trivial. However, the loathing each faction had for the other was burned into their psyche for hundreds of years and it would take a miracle of epic proportions to reconcile the two halves and make them whole again.

    Two figures, well aware it was past curfew, rode through the winding street along the wall, pausing now and again to wait for the guards to pass on their rounds. The figures blended well with the darkness and rode with purpose. Finally, after the slow progression, they stopped next to a tall pole and abandoned their bikes. Climbing to the top of the pole, they lay flat on the platform underneath a large empty billboard, watching for the spotlights to pass over the spot. Once the coast was clear, they got to work, one on each side. After hours of working on the piece, they stepped back and appraised the billboard. Nodding in satisfaction, the figures made it back to their bicycles and rode off in separate directions, each blending into the darker streets of the city as if they never existed.

100 Years Later

Vanessa straightened her shoulders, took a deep breath, and walked into her classroom. The sight that greeted her was not an old one—her students sat in two distinct groups - the Inachis on one side and the Morphosians on the other with a large swath of empty chairs in between. Even after fifty years of reluctant peace, the two sides rarely mingled. They were forced to take the same classes but they expressed their displeasure in numerous ways. After the first few years of integration, the University had taken drastic measures to ensure all classrooms had an equal number of each faction. This had come after most classes in the early days were attended only by the faction members of the particular professor teaching a class. It had been incredibly difficult for students and professors alike.

"Good morning, class," Vanessa said cheerily.

The students stopped their conversations and gave her their attention. Vanessa took another deep breath. Vanessa reached into her bag and pulled out the projector remote. She busied herself with setting it up and organizing her papers. Once everything was in order, she pasted on a smile and turned to the class.

"Right, today we are going to do something a bit different."

A mutter went through the classroom. Vanessa walked over to the light switch and turned off the lights. The projector shone a bright, white light onto the wall behind her. She clicked a button and a black and white picture appeared on the wall. A gasp rippled through the classroom and somebody slammed a hand on their desk.

"What is this?" a student demanded.

Vanessa smiled, "It's ok. Let me explain."

Several students rose from their seats, gathering their things.

"We don't have to stay here for this…"

"I'm going to the dean right now."

"This is madness."

"Please, just let me explain. You are welcome to leave at any time, this is not a mandatory part of your grade," Vanessa tried calming the angry students.

"Why don't we hear her out," one of the students said above the din.

Vanessa heard the students muttering between themselves. Most of them sat back down. One walked down the steps and paused at the door, looking back at his compatriots. Another reluctantly got up and went out with the one at the door. The rest sat in a tense silence, all turning their eyes to Vanessa and waiting.

Vanessa cleared her throat, "Judging by your reactions, you all know what this is…."

The students all nodded in uneasy agreement.

"D'uh," a voice grunted.

The students laughed and Vanessa could feel a little bit of the tension ease in the room. She nodded.

"Would anyone like to explain?"

A hand rose tentatively. Vanessa nodded.

"That... symbol... was first painted on two sides of a billboard by an unknown person in the tenth month of the year of the Sliver Moon of nine twenty-four," Melissa, a fourth-year student stated.

Vanessa nodded, "Very good. Does anyone know why it is important?"

Another student rose, "It began the... Peace."

The Inachi faction expressed their displeasure at the word while the Morphosians squirmed in their seats. Neither faction liked discussing what had led to their current cohabitation of Lepi, or the classroom they were in, for that matter. They accepted it as a necessary evil, but it didn't mean they liked it.

Vanessa held up a hand and the room fell silent again. She thought a moment, perusing her students. She could see the curiosity in them and she wanted to open a dialogue between the two factions. She wanted this generation of students to finally understand why they were against each other and how they could bridge the gap in their differences. She wanted the Peace to be real, not a forced way of life. At that moment, she had an epiphany. She'd decided on a different path for the lesson but she was nothing if not adaptable.

"The Peace has been difficult. The Inachi and Morpho politicians have done their best, but I'm not sure they really understand how to make it better. You, however, have the tools - curiosity, determination, diplomacy—to make it work. To bring harmony to Lepi and the whole country of Doptera."

Melissa raised her hand and spoke when Vanessa acknowledged her, "How? Why us?"

"You've taken the first steps. You are in this classroom. You stayed when others left. You are listening to me, even after I told you it was not detrimental to your grade if you left," Vanessa explained.

The students looked at each other and nodded. One or two shrugged and leaned forward, now hanging on her every word. They wondered what she would say next. She could see the hesitance in a few eyes. She looked up at the image behind her. She gave herself a pep talk. *It's now or never. They either leave all at once in protest or they stay and actually try. You won't know until you propose it.*

"Mrs. Cardui?" Melissa prompted.

Vanessa turned back to her students.

"The image you see is a message from someone. We never knew who made it but the message is clear. The presence of one Inachi wing and one Morpho wing on the same entity is meant to show that they are two halves of the same whole. The two factions working together. The presence of this image was the first of its kind Lepi had ever seen. Some called it treasonous. Others called it a wake-up call. We don't know the original intent but we do know it sparked negotiations between the two factions and brought us to where we are today. My question to you is—could it take us further?"

The students whispered amongst themselves, some glancing across the aisle at the other faction. They shook their heads, not grasping what the professor actually wanted them to do. Another student got up and left the room, clearly not enjoying the direction the class had taken.

"Students, I promise you, if you take on this assignment, your lives will be changed for the better. You can affect the world in which you live. Do you really want the current tensions to remain in Lepi—or do you want real peace?"

"Peace," Melissa said loudly, then shrunk in her seat at the chuckle from the other students.

"I agree," another student said.

A chorus of agreement arose from both factions. Vanessa looked over the students and silently counted them, pleased that she counted an even number on each side.

"Do you trust me?" she asked the class.

"Not really," came a reluctant reply and the class chuckled again.

Vanessa chuckled. "Fair enough. Let me just say—trust each other. Listen to each other. Now, I want each of you to pair off with a student from the other faction. One Inachi and one Morpho in each group."

Vanessa held up her hand as the grousing started. She waited and watched as no one moved. Then, Melissa got up and walked over to an Inachi girl. She held out her hand.

"I'm Melissa," she introduced herself.

The girl looked around in panic for a moment, then sat up straight with determination, holding out her hand, "Io."

From that first introduction, the other students began pairing off. It was tense at first but as more of the students found a partner, the noise in the room grew with introductions and polite conversation. Vanessa waited until the students seemed more comfortable mingling then cleared her throat. The students sat down next to each other, a feat she would have thought impossible before that very moment.

"Now, in the spirit of the symbol behind me, I want you to find out as much as you can about each other's culture. Find out what makes you similar, what makes you different. Work together as the wings in the symbol would have to work together to carry the weight of the body. Find a middle ground. It won't be easy but I know you can do it. Come to me if you have any problems. We will meet again in two weeks. Class dismissed."

Melissa turned to Io and smiled. Io smiled back, somewhat perplexed as to what the assignment was actually about. They did not have to write a paper? Just... talk?

"She's so weird," Io said.

Melissa laughed. "I know, right? My sister took this course two years ago and she said it was a breeze but she never mentioned any assignment like this one."

"My sister took this course two years ago as well!" Io exclaimed.

Melissa laughed. "I would ask her name but I doubt they spoke to each other even if they were in the same class."

"Probably not," Io agreed.

Melissa grabbed a piece of paper out of her notebook and wrote down her contact information. She handed it to Io, who took it and nodded.

"I have another class right now but why don't we schedule a meeting to talk about the assignment?" Melissa asked.

"Sounds good. I'll call you... tonight?"

Melissa nodded. Io nodded and smiled back. It was hard not to catch the bubbly energy from Melissa and it made Io feel more at ease. Melissa gathered up her things and practically skipped out of the room. Io met Vanessa's eyes and raised her eyebrows, daring the teacher to point out the obvious connection the two girls felt. Vanessa shook her head and looked away, giving Io the chance to leave the room.

"That's so odd! Why do you have to do that again?" Melissa giggled.

Io shrugged. "Tradition? Honestly, I have no idea. It is old fashioned and it really makes no sense anymore but we do it anyway."

"I get it, we do things that are obsolete as well but, hey—

whatever makes the family happy!" Melissa wiggled her eyebrows.

Io laughed. She and Melissa had been getting to know each other over several meetings and she found that she genuinely liked the girl. They had much more in common than either girl would have ever thought. In fact, their only differences lie in the way they worshipped their respective gods. Truthfully, even their gods sounded the same—except for different names. The rules of their religions were pretty much the same. The more they spoke, the more they realized the error of the hatred between their factions.

"Mrs. Cardui isn't such a moron after all." Io suddenly became serious.

"What?" Melissa sobered.

"She... she knew this would happen. All it takes is talking and being honest with one another."

Melissa thought a moment, her eyes growing wide. "It's true! If you had asked me a month ago what I thought of the Inachi, I would not have anything nice to say!"

"Nor I of the Morphosians," Io confessed.

"I think this is what that symbol was trying to show everyone—we are all the same, we just need to work together. We need to stop blindly hating one another and learn from each other. The started it a hundred years ago but they didn't really follow through. They only went halfway towards the Peace. We need to make it a lasting peace."

Io thought a moment and nodded. "I have an idea."

Vanessa walked through the hall towards her classroom, growing more concerned at each step. More students than normal lined the hallway and were staring at her. She wondered if she was about to be fired. She knew the rumor mill spread quickly and most of the time she was ignored except by her own students. As she got closer to her classroom, the sheer number of people in the hallway became difficult to navigate. Finally, she reached her door and the students blocking the doorway stepped aside and let her through. The classroom she was met with was very different from the one she had stepped into two weeks prior. Every seat was filled and students were lined up around the edges. It was standing room only. Inachi and Morphosian students mingled in the seats - there was no longer a delineation between the two factions. She approached the lectern cautiously and the classroom became so quiet one could hear a pin drop.

"What's... ahem... what is this all about?" she asked expectantly.

Melissa and Io stood up and approached their professor. She smiled tentatively at them and was stunned at the bright smiles each girl gave her.

"May we?" Melissa asked.

Vanessa nodded and stepped aside. The girls looked at each other and nodded. They unzipped their sweaters to reveal the symbol of one butterfly with folded wings—one Inachi and one Morpho. Vanessa looked in open-mouthed shock at the two girls.

"Fellow students?" Io said to the people assembled in the room.

All the other students shed sweaters and jackets to reveal the same shirts Melissa and Io wore. Vanessa gasped and her eyes teared up.

"Mrs. Cardui, we've learned that whether you were born Inachi or Morpho, we all worship the same gods. We follow the same rules and laws. We come from the same order. We are cut from the same cloth," Melissa said.

"We can respect our differences, celebrate them even, and yet we can still be friends. We can work together to tear down the wall in Lepi and let our cultures strive together rather than falter apart. You told us we can affect change. The student of Lepi University chose to change our world. For the better!" Io exclaimed as she grabbed Melissa's hand and thrust their conjoined hands in the air.

The students in the classroom and those in the hall erupted in cheers. Melissa and Io led the students out into the hallway and into the quadrangle. There, they rose banners flying the symbol as more and more students poured out of the classroom buildings to join the impromptu festivities.

The students began a campaign to force the Inachi and Morpho leaders to talk to one another. Eventually, both sides sat down and really listened to each other. The wall was torn down and the two halves of the sacred city of Lepi were whole again. A miracle had indeed happened. The era of The Lasting Peace had begun in Doptera.

On that day, Vanessa Cardui sat on the floor of her bedroom and cried. She wasn't sad about the state of affairs, she was just sad her grandmother wasn't alive to see it. She pulled a box out from under the bed. A picture lay on top of the box. It was of a beautiful, young Morphosian woman and a tall Inachi man holding hands. The love in their eyes was evident even though the picture had faded. Two bicycles lay at their feet. Behind them, a large billboard was spray-painted with a symbol—a butterfly with one Inachi and one Morpho wing. One had to look closely, but in doing so, could just make out the remnants of black paint on the intertwined hands.

MODERN ART
BY MARSHALL MILLER

The dark clad Grand Inquisitor stepped into his Special Room as he had done countless times before. He had named it the Special Room as he liked the mystery and questions this identifier prompted in people's mind. Questions such as why was it Special? What activities occurred in the room made it 'Special' in the true sense of the word? If the Grand Inquisitor gave it another title, why then its supposed purpose would have been revealed to the masses. Using specific words like interrogation, questioning, interviewing, all words with their own particular weights and meanings, subtracted any chance at mystery when applied to the room. Where was the sense of accomplishment or discovery in that action? Thus the only people who knew the purpose of the Special Room were the Special Room Security, himself, and of course, those invited into this unique space.

So the person known only as the Grand Inquisitor nodded at the two security officers and entered the room. The automatic door was keyed to his being and slid open, then closed with nary a touch from anyone. In the center of the room was a comfortable padded chair. In the single piece of furniture of the Special Room sat a man. The man did not move as the Grand Inquisitor entered. For he had been directed by the security officers not to rise from or leave the chair unless instructed. Others who had not heeded those instructions were beaten by the security officers until they understood the need to follow instructions. While the masses might not know by name or formal definitions the purpose or rules of the Special Room, there were rumors and leaks even in the most controlled of societies. Thus, the man sat.

The statuesque Grand Inquisitor walked into the windowless room, illuminated by a soft pastel light. The walls were painted a warm and calming blue, and some soft music played over the hidden speakers. The creator and owner of the room stopped a few steps in front of the seated man and smiled. The Grand Inquisitor had been told he had a warm and friendly smile. However, that opinion voiced by certain people was viewed by him as suspicious.

"Anton LeMarche," the Grand Inquisitor said in a cheery tone. "I hope that chair is comfortable. I do know the discomfort of having to wait in an uncomfortable chair, especially if a person is no longer young."

Anton LeMarch smiled at the Grand Inquisitor, for they had met many times before at various social functions. Although not real friends, it could be said they were friendly.

"No problem, Sir," replied the older and gray beard man. "I have not waited long, based on my own internal clock. When brought in, I thought my wait would be hours… even days."

The Grand Inquisitor stepped closer as he grinned. "You have now revealed that you are a recipient of many an unfounded rumor, Sir. For I have never kept anyone here for days."

Anton smiled as he replied. "You know how it is, Sir. We, common people, gossip, and then exaggerate."

The Grand Inquisitor frowned as he spoke. "You, Anton LeMarche, Artist, a commoner? Never. You forget my knowledge of your art."

And with that, the wall to Anton's right and the Grand Inquisitor's left became transparent, a window into another room. In that space was a long series of paintings and sculptures. Anton's eyebrows rose in surprise as he saw so many of his works in one place.

"Sir, I must ask," the creative said. "How many of those are originals, and how many are reproductions? I have not seen this many of my endeavors in one place since…"

"Since the State Dinner in your honor two years ago."

"Yes! I had forgotten. And you, Grand Inquisitor, organized it in my honor."

"Which brings us to why you are here today, Anton."

A 3-D sculpture was brought closer to the transparent wall by some unseen force. It was an image of a being, its gender challenging to identify as the head, and upper features were covered by a dark red hood. The face entirely obscured by shadows, the right claw-like hand presented, nay shoved an ever-changing object of light and dark towards the viewer. The object in the hand at first seemed circular, then rectangular, then a prism, next a blob. Mixed in with the light and darkness were blood red hues, then maroons and purples. However, the object was ever changing, there being no discernable pattern.

"I must say, Anton, I find this recent piece of yours exquisite." The nearly supreme official then paused. "However, it presents a problem."

"What is that my respected admirer?" replied Anton.

"It is not the visual effects you have created. My Lord, they are genius. No pattern, ever-changing, almost quantum in nature." The owner of the Special Room then again paused as he observed the ever-shifting hues and shapes. Then he spoke again. "But your genius outdid itself this time. For you incorporated subliminal messages using ultrasonics, somehow interwoven with the shifting visuals."

"Why yes I did, Sir. For I wanted not only for people to see and thus feel the impact of my work, but also to THINK. I wanted those art appreciating Citizens to be tickled in their reasoning portions of their cortex in a specific manner.'

"And that manner was to question. Question what the viewers see, what they hear, what they feel."

"Of course, Grand Inquisitor, you saw to the center of my art piece. Probably during the first minutes of your observing it, yes?"

"Yes. For that is my reason for being, Anton. To observe and inquire, to keep this Most Perfect Union functioning."

"But Sir. I only want our people to use their cognitive abilities so as not to become staid robots. We must have The Order and Structure we developed decades ago, after the Anarchy. All Citizens realize that reality."

The Grand Inquisitor walked around behind the chair and figure. Anton could not turn in the chair as the high padded arms and back restricted movements. Thus, once the Grand Inquisitor was directly to the rear of him, Anton could turn his head to look to the sides, but no further. The music gone, there was complete silence, other than Anton's own breathing and heartbeat in his ears as he became concerned.

When the Grand Inquisitor spoke and broke the extended

silence, Anton jerked in the chair,

"And so the question must be asked: Is this art transformative?" the special official continued. " If not ubiquitous or autonomic but instead a flash point for whatever comes after it... is this art actually an act of revolution?"

Anton nervously licked his lips before he spoke.

"You misunderstand..." His comment was cut off by a tight beam of energy from the ceiling. Anton squealed with pain as his right ear was singed.

"Anton, I am most sorry. I do believe you were about to question my ability to understand."

Anton rubbed his injured ear, then slowly spoke.

"A poor choice of words, Grand Inquisitor. If I, as the artist failed in the attempt to convey a specific idea, feeling, or concept, then I have presented a flawed piece of art. Please allow me to apologize and remedy..."

"But you said, Anton, your purpose was to awaken specific thought processes in our Citizens."

"Sir, again, possibly a poor choice of words..."

"No, wait. You're right. That was *my* poor choice of words. You said to use cognitive abilities, not awaken them." The Grand Inquisitor frowned as he continued. "But then, Anton, you talked about our Citizens becoming robots as if Order somehow damaged the Citizens ability to function. As if 'robot' was a dirty word."

"Sir, I was just trying to produce art that stimulates the Citizens to use there intellect rather than stagnate."

"Our robotic expertise has become a great trade item with other societies and worlds. It has been a boon to our existence since the Anarchy."

The Grand Inquisitor stood still, and Anton began to sweat profusely.

"You know, Anton. I think that figure you so aptly created is an allegory of me. A most exquisite allegorical image of me."

Anton sat still, confused as to how to answer.

"But, the question I have is, in the left hand behind the figures back. What does it conceal?"

"Conceal, my Lord? I had not, in all honesty, given it much thought…"

"Well, then, my good Anton, let me then explain what I, if I am the model for this fantastic piece of art, would have behind my back."

Anton thought he heard a sound like someone pulling a loose-fitting cork from a bottle. The Grand Inquisitor then stepped back around the chair to stand in front of Anton and presented what was in his left hand.

"Peek –A- Boo," the detached head of the Grand Inquisitor said as it grinned, not a dark brown hair out of place.

The two female Special Security Officers outside the door tried not to laugh as a scream came over their communicator earpieces, then was abruptly cut off.

The Grand Inquisitor had such a wicked sense of humor sometimes.

WHAT HAPPENS NEXT
BY ELIZA LOEB

I used to wonder how far this nation will go if we allow the folks in power to keep a morally corrupt president in office. In Donald J. Trump's four year term, I have seen countless offences committed under the guise of false patriotism. Internment camps have been filled beyond capacity, beyond what is considered humane without clean drinking water or toiletries, while its residents are treated like nothing more than senseless beasts. And this is only scratching the surface. President Donald J. Trump idolizes Hitler in ways that I can't even imagine. He presses his ideals on others, forces protestors out in the cold and even makes fun of Autistic reporters. And that was during his first year of presidency. I constantly see people commenting on things that speak out against him and offences that he has made toward women and non-white folk. More often than not, the most common is "Fake News". His biggest atrocity, however, is interning immigrants and having ICE go to the homes of immigrants who sought nothing more than asylum from their countries of origin. But he's not going for the white European immigrants. He's going for the Latinx, the Syrian, the Iranian and more. He is doing what Bush senior had put into motion and Bush Junior had acted upon. He is using fear tactics and propaganda to spread lies and hate about a specific group of people and he knows what effect it will have. He knows how his supporters will react and how they as his followers will make an attempt to militarize and oppress these people to no avail.

  During my time in Virginia, I have obtained employment at Colonial Williamsburg, added a new partner to my family, and said new partner had obtained employment at the Jamestown settlement. And what we have noticed at both of those locations is this: The interpreters and the beliefs that both places have portrayed are entirely different compared to one and other. Colonial Williamsburg not only serves as a living history museum like Jamestown, but it is also the campus location of the college of William and Mary. Many of William and Mary's alumni like wearing MAGA caps and pressing their political beliefs onto others. I remember sitting in Panera with Kayti, my new partner and over hearing a couple of young women talking about the point of civil rights. They continuously questioned "What's the point of it?" and would make passing comments like "Maybe the Civil Rights Act should be abolished. We don't need it." I wanted to rise up. I wanted to say something, but my main concern was with Kayti. My main concern was about how she would feel if I made a public spectacle of myself. She was already having a bad day as was. She didn't want for it to get any worse. So I asked if she would like to leave, and we left. And to this day I still see many people like those women. Donning their MAGA caps and looking down their nose at others they deem lesser. And I continue to wonder, just how many more people will be targeted. How much more will America unravel as a country and how many more people will die just to obtain the ideals of the few. It's not the America that I was promised growing up. It's not the America that the American citizens need. And the back bone of this country was made up of immigrants. Many from China, Italy, Spain, Ireland, Scotland, Russia, France and so on. Its backbone thrives on the people trying to make a life for themselves... or at least it used to. Now, we have to worship those who were born with a silver spoon in their mouth. Those who have never had to work a day in their lives. And it angers me. It angers me that a bunch of white guys in office have so much while everyone else has so little. And it angers me that many of the white Americans that come in to Yorktown or Jamestown find the information they obtain completely and utterly pointless. And it's because of them that we have the bastard in office. It's because of them that "Immigrant Detention Centers" are packed beyond capacity with little food or water or even basic hygiene components. And I fear what they will do to those people and I begin to think of a book that I had read once. And many of them are likely thinking the same thing that many of the characters in said book had thought. "Why me?"

There have been many occasions where I have seen history repeat its self. And there are many who believe that history is just history and that it means nothing. The united states of America is hardly as united as it used to be. Its beginnings were good. The separation of church and state was good. Because it meant that one could be allowed to press their religious beliefs upon another person for the sake of a political agenda. Yet, here we are. Abortion is being made illegal, women are being arrested for miscarriages and losing babies to gunshot wounds. These women have done absolutely nothing wrong. These people trying to cross the border and seeking asylum, have done nothing wrong. It is not illegal to seek asylum. It should not be illegal to have a miscarriage. But it should be illegal to wrongfully incarcerate an entire group of people. It should be illegal to neglect the people you lead because they are not wealthy. And it *should* be illegal to deny benefits to families and folks in need for the sake of lining your own or some other billionaire's pockets.

And so I wonder....

How many more will be arrested? How many more people will be put in to an internment camp if nothing is done right away? How many more people will wonder if they will live to see tomorrow?

And as I look at the world as it is today, I wonder. I remember the meaning of the word tyranny. I know what an internment camp looks like. I know what genocide and war looks like.

America as we know it is at the seventh stage of genocide, and there is only a few more stages to go before the government tries to cover it up and deny that it even happened.

I exhaust myself in trying to make sense of it all. I hate that what is happening now is similar to Nazi Germany and the burning of roam. Although I don't feel that the current POTUS knows how to play any instruments seeing as the only talent that he actually has is running his mouth, and he can't even do that well. I especially exhaust myself over how many will hear about this time period. Will it be seen as just *another bad presidency*? Or will children and adults stop and actually learn from it?

These are the sort of things that go through the head of someone whose citizenship can be taken away in any point in time. And having been born on Guam, that time may be soon. And then maybe I will end up in a concentration camp, myself.

With where this country is headed, guarantees are but a fools game. You live, you breath, you watch and you learn.

AMERICAN ELEGY
BY SHEILA MENGERT

Abraham Cardozo had a problem. Since his graduation from law school four years ago everything in America had seemed to go into freefall. Everywhere there was contention and an abiding nastiness broadcast at full volume from the various absolutist discourses and narratives, each contending for supremacy. Some of these claims were religious in nature, others political, and others still simply the fracas bred of contending egos seeking attention on social media.

"I am living in the age of the *prima donna*," Abraham said to himself in the course of the inner narrative that each of us possesses as we try and make some sense of the world and fill our fleeting hours with at least some measure of stability and satisfaction. Abraham's mind was disturbed by events. Everything had become so strident, rising in pitch and volume to a sustained squeal like the sound of microphone feedback at a rock concert.

Among other items of note it was the fiftieth anniversary of the Stonewall Inn Riot that by 2019 had become the LGBT equivalent of the shots that rang out between British and American troops at Concord Bridge in 1776. Rainbow Flags were expected to be flown everywhere in celebration of the event and of the full emergence of LGBT rights on the world stage from sleepy villages in Botswana to Greenwich Village in New York where it all seemed to have begun one summer night.

Meanwhile in the world of beleaguered heterosexuals various petitions were circulating to keep drag queens out of libraries where they had lately been introduced as purveyors of a so-called story hour, just one more instance of the nefarious effort to normalize the unspeakable among the young in the view of various religious groups. Disorder was everywhere. Across the vast Pacific Ocean an American and a Russian ship had barely avoided a collision in the South China Sea. The food situation in North Korea was growing more threatening each day due to poor harvests and the sanctions that remained in place even after the "lover's meetings" between Donald Trump and Kim Jung Un. In Europe Brexit looked inevitable and it seemed quite possible that noble England might be heading for a reprise of the post World War II style rationing if its economy should collapse. Below the border, Mexico had avoided tariffs for now by agreeing to act as a more efficient buffer between the fleeing hordes of refugees from Honduras and Guatemala and the safe harbor of America. At the bottom of the world in Antarctica great ice shelves were calving daily into the southern seas off Patagonia. The yearly forest fires had already started in California. In the internecine conflicts between liberals and conservatives within the Catholic Church a statement had been issued by some Bishops in Kazakhstan to remind the diminishing number of church-going Catholics, let alone the remarried and sexually rebellious, to toe the line or risk the consequences. Rain was still causing flooding in the American mid-west and south. Only Vice-President Mike Pence seemed at ease as he looked up with hound-dog-like devotion to the all-wise Commander-in-Chief (and a hell of a golfer) Donald Trump.

Things were being shaken up everywhere it seemed. Everybody was yelling at everybody and Abraham Cardozo, product of reason and tolerance, felt compelled at last to intervene. Abraham Cardozo put on his glasses to read over the text of what he hoped would be of some use in the political struggles of the present hour. A little effort on his part he felt, a little cool judicial reasoning and all could be put right. What was called for at this critical hour was an *amicus brief* to unmask the catastrophic trend of the Trump agenda of spurious populism masking corporate rule.

Abraham, as we will familiarly refer to him rather than by the august name of Cardozo (no actual blood relation to the famous jurist) like many Americans of this particular time and place was suffering from the confusion bred from the daily deluge of events. Each new day brought its own spate of revelations, assessments and counter-assessments in the endless factional currents and entrenched interests of America. Like many of his generation he had been accustomed to the concept of on demand services and the ability to remove the unpleasant and the intolerable by simply hitting the delete button on whatever device was handy. Reality might be virtual or actual depending upon one's underlying view of metaphysics, but in any case it should be subject to framing and manipulation. If Abraham had learned anything in law school it was to present the facts, whatever they might be, encased in an overall narrative that would lead a jury to adopt the client's point of view. Facts were flexible like the space-time continuum; they merely provided the field that could, if skillfully presented, lead to a favorable verdict. As in the reaction to the New Criticism by the post-modernists, it was all a matter of point of view. No text could be expected to speak for itself under changing conditions. The young attorney almost feared to read what he had just composed though because he was aware of the utter transiency of all narratives and the lack of a common point of reference for meaning and relevance.

The provisional text of his manuscript read as follows:

No narrative can hope to exist in utter isolation from a receptive community that can at once be its audience and the source of its relative value assessment among similar discourses. This is the first step along the journey towards general acceptance as truth. As discourses have increased in number and variety the communities that can receive them have similarly fragmented so that a general sense of meaning is absent.

As an example of this truth, Thomas Wolfe, the great American novelist, is famous for saying that you can't go home again. This phrase has always had for me a certain nostalgic ring because it implied that one was caught in the dilemma of desiring to return to a predictable and unified world but were doomed to rejection and misunderstanding, as though exile contained within itself a just punishment for ever having left home in the first place: abandon us and we will abandon you. As the years have passed however I have come to see things differently. Thomas Wolfe was simply making a statement of fact: the reason that we cannot go home again is that home no longer exists as it has been preserved in our memory after long absence. The accuracy of memory is such that it preserves images and structures in all of their former integrity long after those structures may have altered or ceased to exist. We assume a set of relations in space and time to endure so that although *we* may have changed *they* remain locked and frozen, just waiting for us to take them up again.

We even go so far as to apply this standard to people and

to resent the temerity of their daring to grow and to change even as we have. We thought to return from a long expedition, laden down with dromedaries of wisdom, riches, experience, and in possession of triumph while they, poor things, could only stand looking outwards into the barren distance awaiting our return. After all, we Americans judge progress always in a comparative sense: there is no such thing as prosperity until it can be held up against a standard of deprivation and penury. This is why Americans are so jealous and afraid that those just below them will move marginally up the ladder of social or economic status. Meanwhile we grant *carte blanch* privileges to the upper classes to pursue their lives of indulgence without fear or even the burden of our resentment at their good fortune. We may even derive a certain degree of reflected glory from our native aristocrats so that when Donald Trump refers to other nations as "Shit-hole countries" rather than as "developing nations" his avid followers can congratulate themselves and agree, *"They shore as hell are!"*

      In the year of 2019 then when everything remains suspended and the great and hoped-for deliverance of 2020 (when pray God we will see clearer and return our nation to some measure of sanity) it is becoming ever clearer that we can't go home again. Integrity is that quality that bestows identity and we have pawned it for a short pay-day loan. Imagine if you will if the various qualities and characteristics of a substance should become suddenly lacking in that adhesiveness that creates order and security. This adhesiveness goes by various names but in law it is called precedent and the stricture of tradition that precedent imposes is called *stare decisis*. It is not that the past is always wiser than the present; the rule is imposed for another purpose entirely. The conservation of precedents creates what may be called the body of the law. Theoretical structures such as contract and tort are elaborately balanced and highly evolved relationships of multiple factors just as living organisms are. Precedents are the genetic mutations that when selected and preserved over time finally evolve into the extended predicates of the law. So it is that when mere political rhetoric is willing to cast this bastion of order aside in order to secure short-term gains it is a warning that civilization is tottering and the eyes of hungry beasts in the outer darkness begin to glitter.

  It is not the advent of Donald Trump that is so appalling, America has known the temporary triumph of vulgar opportunists before this; the thing that terrifies me is the readiness with which approximately one-third of our fellow citizens are prepared to surrender everything upon which democracy is based simply to get their long-deferred wish-list met. It shows that a significant number of Americans have no idea of what such cherished terms as due process and basic honesty mean. This is why each new fantastic claim or instance of personal abuse to his enemies or former enablers is becoming less shocking over time as the President proceeds in his one-of-a-kind Presidency. Each impact further dulls our sense of propriety and decency so that the public sphere now smells like the abandoned stall of a fishmonger. It is all so familiar to anyone who has ever studied the gradual consolidation of power under Adolf Hitler. I keep waiting for Nancy Pelosi to appear, tear-stained on the evening news, as she looks up at the smoking ruin of the Capitol Building. So it isn't that we cannot go home again: the problem is that our home has been disintegrating before us every day since 2016…

With the prospect of his annual visit to the Oregon coast for his vacation in the offing Abraham decided before he left Seattle to put the matter of his proposed literary intervention before his old con/law instructor for a provisional opinion. He waited for an answer while Professor Manuel Cortez, law professor and aficionado of liberation theology, sat back and considered the matter after reading the rough draft.

"Well, that's all that I have so far. What do you think of the general tone?" Abraham queried hopefully, the general sense of awe that former students have for various favorite instructors remained with him still.

"It won't make law review material, but perhaps an op-ed piece."

"I didn't think it sounded like a note for law review; too general and too contemporaneously relevant for that. A public policy review perhaps?"

Professor Cortez considered the suggestion.

"No, not even there, I don't believe. I'm not sure that such a thing exists anymore anyway, commonly rooted public policy I mean. Have you thought of an archeology journal? We may just get the Trump wall after all along our southern border out of all this. It will be a great tourist attraction one hundred years from now, a symbol of our national ethos in decline."

Abraham smiled, "You are being facetious. You think I'm too earnest in writing a piece like this."

"No, I think you are saying what most people think already, but it's too late. Can you see that? You are making a general appeal after the filing date has passed. This whole Donald Trump phenomenon was already foreseeable thirty years ago when education began to break down in this country, maybe even earlier than that. I saw it coming as early as the Bork nomination and the eventual arrival of the Rehnquist Court. Do you remember your Constitutional Law course with me when I pointed out that it all came down to an act of faith. Law is a religion. As soon as the outcome becomes more important than legal due process the whole thing becomes meaningless. It is the unwritten covenant of judicial probity in reasoning that is our only guarantee that civilization will prevail. Law school isn't a trade school; it's a novitiate in the order of a religion called jurisprudence. The students who realize this don't make the most money, but they keep the whole thing alive. You were one of the ones who I thought might keep the old faith going for one more round at least."

Abraham smiled. "I had a head start. Talmud study you know."

The Professor smiled.

"Me too, ever read Canon Law? The Roman Church finds its ultimate principle of order in God, but for the day-to-day work there is always Canon Law to keep the heretics at bay. We both have a healthy respect for the transcendent in our religious traditions but we know that in its pure form only the mystics try and deal with the transcendent dimension directly. For the rest of us there is only the comfort provided by doctrine and by law. When you break the laws you plead guilty and hope for a reduced sentence on the other side. We call it Confession."

"So you think that religion is comparable to the criminal law?" Abraham asked.

"It started there, remember the forbidden fruit? Of course that presumes a historical reading of the text of Genesis."

"Is there another way to read it?"

The Professor considered the question before explaining.

"What if you read the text like an example of the Wisdom Literature, more like the Book of Job or Proverbs? What if you look at it like a novel by Franz Kafka describing the human predicament and the dangers of premature acquaintance with moral questions that we haven't the strength to confront or to surmount? By reading the creation account in Genesis as an historical text all sorts of problems emerge that are otherwise avoidable. Christian history is awash in the consequences of what may have been an initial misreading by assigning the text to an inappropriate genre and distorting authorial intent in the process. I'm not saying I am right, mind you, but if the study of law teaches us one key skill it is to dispute established precedents."

"I thought lawyers were the bulwark of established interests," Abraham commented dryly.

"Only Republican lawyers," answered Professor Cortez archly.

Abraham Cardozo reflected.

"Then Donald Trump is not a revolutionary populist after all."

Professor Cortez sat back in his chair and placed his finger tips together as of old. He proceeded at last as he had once done in the classroom.

"Trumpism ... and I speak of it as an institution rather than as the individual political program of one man (it is more like an opportunistic infection) is a strategy rather than a movement. Its guiding principle is to win power and to retain it for as long as possible. I watched in the primaries as the various Republican contenders for the Presidential nomination in 2016 fell by the wayside like so many straw men and suddenly it dawned on me that they had misunderstood both the temper of the times and what the Presidency as an institution has become for all of us. You see Abraham we don't elect Presidents on the basis of qualifications and intelligence any more but on their ability to confirm our prejudices, to flatter our dreams, and to alleviate our anxieties. Donald Trump realized long ago as a speculator that from the perspective of the buyer symbols are more important than substance. What is the whole Trump Empire but an example of leveraged illusions? It's all about branding. Donald Trump may be the first President who considers living in the Whitehouse to be slumming. That's why he is always off to Mar-a-Lago. By the way, the name means: "sea to lake." The resort forms a bridge between the sea and the Intracoastal Waterway. In the same manner Trumpism bridges traditional conservatism with the illusion of a populist revolution from below. You get the best of both worlds. You can be a stodgy, fundamentalist, climate-change denying, rapture-awaiting, religious conservative and you can be a rich Plutocrat ready to dump the last shovel-full of earth onto the grave of the American middle-class. You can be an out and out bigot ready to scare black folk back to carefully policed ghettos. You can be a woman who thinks that ill-mannered and dominant men are a turn-on. You can in fact be anyone who wants to clock-in on a vicarious win to keep from the dawning suspicion that indebted America could collapse at any moment and follow the British Empire into the annals of past glory. You can be any of these and Donald Trump is your man. In politics rhetoric is everything; it even trumps truth."

"And the other candidates didn't realize this?" Abraham inquired.

Professor Cortez laughed.

"They thought they were competing for a job interview. They showed up with lengthy resumes and lots of earnestness and Trump made mincemeat out of them because only he realized that Presidential elections are a game-show. When the voter steps behind the curtain, he hopes that the box that he chooses will contain a new car and not a hundred cans of minced squid."

Abraham considered. "What about impeachment?"

"That might seem the best course constitutionally speaking, but only if you want another four years of Trump."

"I don't understand," Abraham looked puzzled.

"Really, what have we just been talking about? Trump is a master of leveraging. By handing him an impeachment that will not be confirmed in the Senate the House of Representatives would be giving him the one boost that he needs to come back as a winner in "season two." I am sure that Nancy Pelosi, smart lady that she is, knows this. Her task is to let the horses rear but keep them attached to the chariot. Once impeachment breaks loose Trump wins and he knows it; he even invites it. The one thing that the great egoist can't stand is sustained suspicion. It's like swamp-gas percolating up from the ground on the fairway of a golf course, not fatal but annoying, and Donald Trump is not accustomed to being annoyed. He wants a quick victory not a sustained campaign because in a sustained campaign actual results matter. What has he to show for the first years of his Presidency?"

The Professor continued, counting his points off on his fingers.

"No wall built, no new health care plan, a tax deal that has added over two trillion dollars to the national debt, a runaway stock-market just begging for a correction, a series of trade-wars that are bankrupting farmers, a love-affair with the fat-kid ruling North Korea who is running out of patience while his people starve under sanctions, and a lot of alienated allies from Japan to England. All Trump has to run on is his assumed victimhood and all the Progressive Wing of the Democratic Party wants to do is to hand that cherished status back to him on a silver platter by impeaching him when he only has one effective year to go in his ill-advised Presidency. Believe me Abraham, the calliope of the whole Trump circus is running out of steam: the rhetoric is getting threadbare, the promises are unfulfilled, and people are tired of his jejune name-calling. The whole thing is just one more mortgage loan on Debtor America. The real answer is to give the man free rein and wait it out. The one person who can defeat Donald Trump is Donald Trump. Otherwise…"

"Otherwise?" Abraham asked.

Professor Cortez shrugged his shoulders.

"Well think about moving to Denmark or New Zealand."

This was the context of the reflections that pursued Abraham Cardozo as he headed out to the Oregon coast for his annual recuperation from his fourth year of practicing law in a small eight-person Admiralty firm. He had drifted towards Admiralty Law because it allowed him to place daguerreotypes of Clipper Ships on his office wall and to practice in Federal Court rather than in the squalid state courts so often reminiscent of the world of Charles Dickens' fog-shrouded London with prisoners in orange suits being arraigned and quarreling couples fighting over their children. It was comforting to apply law to stately collisions between vessels and personal injury claims under the Jones Act. But he was tired, chronically tired as most attorneys are, and it was always a joy to slip the traces, to pass his caseload on to another lawyer, and to seek the open sea again.

There are many routes out to the Oregon Coast but Abraham preferred the slow road down from Aberdeen to the Columbia River and across the bridge to Astoria. On trips like this Abraham was accustomed to undertaking that most neglected of pastimes, introspection and retrospection; the search for what Thomas Wolfe had called "the last lane-end into heaven." The ethos of America was never explored so vividly as in the novels and short-stories of that most neglected of America's great 20th century novelists. Seventeenth century prose evidently did not play well with the staccato rhythms of mid-century America. But perhaps it was Wolfe's sense of the tragic that did not sit well among a nation always avid for the next cheap delight. Faulkner had the advantage of comparative incomprehensibility combined with the slow majesty of a funeral dirge in his prose, or perhaps it was Wolfe's youth that worked against him, dying so young at thirty-eight. His disappointments always seemed only proportionate to his hunger which was limitless. He never quite managed that most difficult of authorial tasks: to climb out of one's own skin. It is a task that is spared to the lawyer who always writes within the established texture of the law. There is nothing more intimating than using the elder tongue of language to speak new truths or to devise a new music from old chords.

    Abraham observed the flow of his thoughts as he turned southwards at Aberdeen. The road unspooled before him in the late-spring light of a June day. The southwestern counties of Washington State are comparatively undeveloped. They consist of sloughs and estuaries, of oysters and lumber, salmon and light tourism. The restricted economy creates an aura of migration and abandonment, of boarded up shops and empty pavements. The dollar is the lifeblood of communities such as these and where dollars are lacking everything dries up like a mirage in the desert.

    But these were not the sole basis for Abraham's subdued mood as he threaded the narrow roads between timber cuts and outlooks across the wind-ruffled waters of Willapa Bay. It was rather the sense of passing opportunities that led him into the habitual sense that like his namesake he would always be a wandering Aramean with only the vestigial promise of his various faiths to sustain him. A habit of reflective thought can be a great disadvantage. He had long ago lost the capacity for mob-enthusiasm; his joys were personal and often difficult to explain to others.

    The curves of the road were compelling and hypnotic, yet he wasn't sleepy, only mesmerized by the sense of movement and the passing foliage of the trees. Suddenly the great waters of the Columbia River were before him and then the great high span of the bridge that grants access to the further shore of Oregon. His spirits picked up as they always did when the first sector of his journey was behind him. This was the Oregon land that had inspired the pioneers to cross a continent of plains and desert; this was the goal and the vision.

He stopped for lunch in Cannon Beach and walked the familiar streets munching an apple turnover and looking in the shop windows at summer clothes and trinkets, all part of early family vacations on the coast. He remembered college parties here as well, falling asleep in strange beds with the floor littered with the sleeping bodies of college friends after a night of beer and hilarity, everything swaying like a ship in an unquiet but not stormy sea. Was he that same person still, the one who as yet had everything before him but no clear idea of what anything was really about? How strange that he did not feel at that time the vast vacuum of all that he did not yet know. But then youth brings its own fullness. There is, if nothing else, that expectancy that earth has been awaiting one's particular advent to finally reveal its long deferred promises. Was that what the first Abraham had felt, he the father of peoples?

Upon leaving Cannon Beach the road climbs steadily upwards. At the crest the view south from Neakanie Mountain over the little community of Manzanita down to Tillimook Bay was as always inviting to the wanderer, majestic and intimidating at once, as the land suddenly ends and plunges downwards into the frothing surf. He found himself envisioning the many prairie towns lying behind him and the great Rocky Mountains of Colorado, then the plains, the Mississippi River and the rich, green yet populous eastern states.

This was the America that Trump promised to make great again. Had it ever ceased to be great except in the smallness of our commercial obsessions? Abraham thought of the great Redwood forests, gone in a century, with only a few forlorn representatives remaining in groves around Eureka. The west must have been one vast cathedral then. Surely that was when America was truly great, before the great exploiters ever arrived.

The problem with the command to fill and subdue the earth was that no exact figures were provided. Did filling the earth demand that the other animals should all be in cages or shrink-wrapped in the meat department of big grocery chains? Is there no residual value to frontiers, to untouched wilderness with no exhaust smog obscuring the likes of El Capitan in Yosemite? In reality no one possesses more than a life-estate; the very idea of a fee simple absolute in the most nefarious of legal fictions. And as to future interests the only real reversion is to the bare plot of the grave. He recalled the poet Thomas Gray's *Elegy in a Country Churchyard* and thought again of the current President. Would his empire resemble more that of Shelley's *Ozymandias* "Look on my works ye mighty and despair?"

The sea gives the lie to all such presumption; year in and year out the tides wash immense chasms through volcanic outcroppings. History is dwarfed by geology. "Round the remains of that colossal wreck the lone and level sands stretch far away." The meaning of history is always the creation of some later author long divorced from the original event. We bestow meaning after the fact seeking to find a pattern in random circumstance.

What is the initial impetus that has propelled human life from the beginning? Are we only the latter inheritors of a defunct line about to be transmuted by technology into inorganic hybrids? Should we each patent our particular genome to prevent infringement by some future corporation that will dig up our bones to mine genetic material for splicing into zombies, full scale replicas of ourselves with the brain left out, eyes staring into nothingness but ripe with livers and kidneys to be harvested at will by elite survivors? Will the soul be present in miniature in every fragment of our genetic legacy seeking a lost composite integrity?"

Thus did Abraham the potential father of many people query the changing scene before him and the ocean, mother of all life-forms.

As the afternoon waned Abraham Cardozo passed Tillimook with its green farms and after another half hour had passed crossed over Neskowin Head and entered Lincoln City named for the man who once saved the Union but was viewed by the Confederacy as a tyrant.

"Will there be a Trump Memorial some day in Washington or is there still a little residual room on Mount Rushmore for one more face to rule them all with the great comb-over the best place in America to take a selfie?" Abraham wondered as he headed through town to his hotel. The thought made him smile and his mood began to lighten.

He was home again in the place that was so transient by nature that it would always remain the same. Coastal towns are less aptly described as cities than they are as encampments, temporary refuges before the great waters. No doubt there were traditions and old families here, but for Abraham Cardozo one of the chief charms of the coast was its transience and anonymity. There is an advantage to be gained by being a perpetual stranger, the advantage of not entering into the squalor and narrowness of local politics, of not knowing who the movers and shakers are, who constitutes local royalty with a stranglehold on influence and social prominence.

It was good to know that each community was like a separate pearl on a linear strand reaching from Astoria to Brookings on the California border. Abraham had learned from his namesake the danger of occupied settlements with borders to defend. As a practitioner of reformed Judaism he saw that the genius of the Jewish culture lay in its combination of tradition and adaptability. When necessity demanded it tradition became sufficiently cosmopolitan to adapt to changing environments. Personally upon looking back on Jewish history Abraham preferred the Diaspora to Zionism. He left it to the millennial Christian Fundamentalists to salivate over the prospect of Armageddon. Abraham saw nothing wrong with being a 21st century incarnation of the perennial wandering Jew.

It still seemed strange to him that he had ever chosen the law as a profession, but then with a name like Cardozo, no actual relation to the great Justice Benjamin Cardozo, it had seemed the natural course to pursue rather than journalism. Now in the age of so-called fake news when journalists are scorned as "enemies of the people" he was glad he had made this choice. People still maintained a fear or at least a grudging respect for lawyers. No one was quite sure of what going to the law actually entailed but there was a sort of awe reserved for people who can sign a complaint and summon one to court, to file an answer to a lawsuit, submit to the processes of discovery and depositions, and quite possibly to force one to pay reparations or damages to the prevailing party. Lawyers understood where the landmines of liability were located amidst a general plain of mistrust and animosity between various factions in the vast mottled political tapestry of American discontents (to mix about three metaphors). Maybe that was the problem: that no overriding symbol or narrative could ever capture American reality, not even when Twittered each day from the sublime office of the Presidency by a man who claimed to know all of the best words (a boast never put to the test of actual display).

Insofar as there remained any primary residue of value in modes of communication it did not reside in words, metaphors, or even in concepts but rather in the flickering modality of images.

Hearing had given way to the sense of sight – story as transposed from syntax to a mere succession of video frames. Connectivity not of meaning but of mere sequence to produce the desired response was the key to achieving the desired end, a following of likes. The sheer emergence of mass approval equaled power and power translated into money. The companies with the highest capitalization were mere agencies of communication and influence. Marketing had triumphed over the returns of finance, and finance over management. All was a big economy version of the old "rock, paper, scissors game." Bodies were big bucks. Body was metaphor. Body was economic juice. Never underestimate the commercial value of strategically placed and jiggling silicone on the penile responsiveness of the stock market. "Today is today is today! Forget yesterday! And as for tomorrow … by then we will already have changed our position in the endless round of the cultural equivalent of day-trading."

    These were thoughts of Abraham, bright young attorney and aspiring reformer, as he looked down on the beach from the hotel dining room and saw the ever hungry pelicans wheeling about in tight formations over the sapphire hued morning sea.

    "I want to forget these things on my vacation," he said to himself. "I don't even want to see the coverage of Trump's visit to London. Poor Theresa May is on her way out and the shadow of Brexit is nearer every day. I wonder if I will ever get back to St. Ives in Cornwall or to Scarborough in Yorkshire. I miss the pubs, cozy places, friendly folk… Maybe I'll run up to Nye Beach today, have a pint of Guinness stout, look out to the lighthouse on Yaquina Point, settle down a bit and forget national politics…"

    "But events matter surely," returned the omniscient narrator that haunts us all with the recalcitrant points of living in an era that claims to possess ultimate significance, as though the fate of all human life and of the planet itself resided with us by right of temporary possession. That narrative voice is a one without personality but only the x-ray ability to scan thoughts, to strip away mental walls, and to leave us, naked and alone, trapped in the aquarium of written narrative where we swim about like fish bumping into walls seeking escape but seeing only our own reflection in the glass.

The checking in process at his hotel was routine and an hour later Abraham was on the road again. He passed the sleepy little town of Depoe Bay and ascended to the top of Cape Foulweather, named by the redoubtable explorer, Captain Cook. Below the viewpoint stretched the clear expanse of empty space. Abraham could just glimpse the outline of what may have been Cape Perpetua on the furthest margin of his vision looking southwards while below him the kelp forests waved about beneath a frothing green sea.

"I never get tired of this," he said to himself feeling within that inner frisson of delight that can only come with a summer morning by the sea.

"Why don't I stay here always?" he asked himself in that silent dialog of impulse and intentions that are never finally resolved into a sense of complete and lasting happiness so that we push on towards lesser pleasures forgetting that just for a brief moment all desire has ceased in a transient and therefore contradictory nirvana.

Abraham thought of that poem by Wallace Stevens *The Idea of Order at Key West*. Various lines from it came back to him lingering like Proust's Madeleine pastry.

"Imagine a world not littered with mental traces of stray lines by the great poets," he thought. "How do people manage to navigate without such guide-posts for their perceptions?"

He thought again of the wasteland of what must be Donald

Trump's imagination, oozing out its various diatribes of resentment and mediocrity, distilled in order to intoxicate a salacious group of his avid followers. Abraham thought of the Great Plains from Iowa to Arkansas, flooded and tornado-lashed for week after week. But then this was only 2019 and by next year the news cycle will have passed and all have been forgotten.

"But what if there is war with Iran or North Korea?"

Abraham queried the open space of the gradually warming day.

"I will look back on this day and its prospects then and wonder why I wasn't grateful for just this day when my life still lay shining before me."

Abraham pictured the various types of chaos that might break forth from just beyond the ever-receding horizon lying westward from where he now stood. He wondered if there really were dragons in the sea.

"How does this day relate to all that has been before? Will I make a decision today that will make all of my prior plans suddenly lost, superseded, and irrelevant? Some new insight perhaps … some foolish gesture of protest to capture the roving eye of the media, be granted a 15 second manifesto before being locked up for streaking at a MAGA rally?"

He smiled to himself.

"I would rate the honor of a Presidential Tweet! When did we start first start thinking in little corpuscles of expression?"

Maybe that is the problem: thought cannot exist without context. To present an argument in little machine-gun bursts is inherently and methodologically flawed. What would Montaigne have thought of this method of discourse when he wrote his great essays or the great controversialists like Defoe or Voltaire? In our era it is adequate to simply berate the other person, the triumph of the *ad hominum* argument must be supreme.

Abraham shook his head and resumed his survey of the pageant of land, earth, and sky that lay just before him, reflecting that the curvature of the earth limits our perspective from whatever height we are able to attain. The ocean is essentially ungraspable in its full magnificence. Even at sea one is limited to the compass-bound circumference set by the location of the vessel. One sails for days and weeks with no sign of progress and suddenly one has arrived at Old Cathay or the Malayan archipelago with streets crowded with rickshaws and all of the picturesque genius of native handicrafts.

Abraham smiled. The Kiplingesque image vanished only to be replaced by high-rise office buildings and polluted air over vast industrial complexes all churning out goods to be sold on credit to the bottomless appetites of American consumers.

"We simply have a head-start over them rather than keeping them as juridical colonies like the Dutch, the French, and the British," he said to himself.

"Perhaps it will go on and on. Dick Cheney says that deficits don't matter, at least if you are top-dog."

He put on a British manner, "The poor blighters have no choice old man. They don't want to go back to rice-farming. Besides, the almighty dollar is the world's reserve currency. Of course the Americans are a bloody crass race but they always know what they want and find a way to get it. No doubt one day they will decide to have a culture."

Abraham had always been an Anglophile or at least one who adored the American literary aristocracy of New England. He revered Emerson, Thoreau, Hawthorne, and Melville. These exalted the individual and aspired to no greater empire beyond the empire of the possession of one's own soul and integrity. It was hard to say where America had gone wrong, perhaps when the country pushed beyond the Appalachians or built the Erie Canal.

Maybe it was the presumption of the Louisiana Purchase or the Lewis and Clark Expedition that set America on the road to Empire by slaughter and conquest.

In any case America was top-dog and determined to remain such. Still there was the phenomenon of Trumpism which betokened the fear of Americans that they just might lose status or be nudged aside by a billion Chinese or a billion workers from India who would steal their jobs in the few remaining industries that cared to build factories in America. All of that potential future anxiety was focused for now south of the border and within our own hemisphere. Meanwhile the North Koreans were building missiles that could hold the entire west coast of America hostage and China was seeking to establish complete hegemony over the South China Sea. America no longer sought as in the Bush years for a cobbled together "coalition of the willing," now we were determined to go it alone.

Abraham looked for an image that he could use later in his proposed op-ed piece. He thought of the lumbering figure of Donald Trump, the very embodiment of the William Howard Taft school of physical culture for Presidents. He thought of the aggressive yellow comb-over, the pursed lips and squinting eyes, all somehow betraying fear more than actual confidence, rather like a polar bear on a shrinking ice-floe.

He thought of Trump's chief enabler, Senator Mitch McConnell of Kentucky who always looked like he had just eaten too many prunes at breakfast and must seek a swift refuge of retreat. But maybe it wasn't a matter of image but of vision, historical vision into the causes of the fall of empires that was needed today above all else. Could America ever embrace world democracy as opposed to one tilted towards and enabling American exceptionalism?

Abraham doubted it. He wasn't even sure if Americans

wanted freedom in the real political sense. If the truth be told we sort of envied the Chinese even with their hegemonic surveillance state. At least it produced impressive economic growth and everyone had a job. The real image of America, as judged by the Republican vision, was more like this: I am content to work until I drop dead of a heart attack or Jesus comes again as long as I get to keep my non-union job and my gun. When did Americans decide to settle for beads and trinkets from big-box stores rather than for real freedom?

"The first freedom must be the freedom from existential fear." As he reflected upon this realization Abraham understood that American determination to build a wall around itself was a sort of collective confession that we are terrified that the great expanse of morally vacuous and narcissistically indulgent America might better be filled by a more industrious people. The best image of the Trump Presidency was derived from the super-indulgence of his golfing vacations at Mar-a-Lago combined with his plebian taste in the preference for hamburgers.

Before returning to his hotel room in Lincoln City for the night Abraham drove up to Newport. In the quaint old neighborhood of Nye Beach he sat before a meal of corned-beef and potatoes and a pint of frothy Guinness Stout. He was starting to relax at last; it always took him awhile to adapt to the slower rhythms of the coast after the hurly-burley of Seattle. It was hard to disengage from the six-minute interval that the interior meter demands in the regime of billable hour requirements of legal practice.

After his second Guinness the interior rhythm began to flat-line and give way to the long slow pulse-beats of the ocean outside. It was a pleasure to simply look about and see people having a good time around him. The noise of the place was reassuring with its unfocused laughter and talk. This was the

America that Abraham loved, one of leisure and of simple largess. He liked the blend of unconscious ethnicities that made Americans in their heart of hearts naturally hospitable. It had taken years of indoctrination by the devotees of various exclusionary Christian sects anxiously awaiting the separation of the sheep from the goats to close the door of the American mind to other people. America had begun as a secular Republic content to manage the country with the same dignified aloofness that God exercised in the Deist view in managing the universe. The laws of the nation should be as frugal and few as the law of gravity. It was hard to say when things had changed. It was hard to imagine an area of life that was no longer micro-managed by some administrative body or penetrated by some information gathering algorithm. It was a relief for Abraham to be effectively off-line for a time.

Freedom in the last analysis may be summed up as the right to disengage. Instead of seeing freedom as a prelude to action perhaps it is better conceived as the ability to do nothing, simply to listen to the great base-undertone of existence. When did Americans forget the value of silence? What were the great prairies like when they harbored only the soft sighing of the wind through the long-grasses? No wheat or soy-beans then but rather only the unbroken sod and the grazing bison. What were the Oregonian seas like when the salmon thrived and the whales had yet to be hunted for lamp-oil? Could any of this natal largess ever be restored? Each day brought new studies of species extinctions before the sheer onrush of human expansion and development.

Disengagement at one time was thought of as the equivalent of alienation, of loss of community, to risk being an outcast or to be viewed as a malcontent; but that was in the days when conformity was seen as the equivalent of virtue. Now to disengage seemed the only way to maintain one's individual sanity. Collective America appeared to be committed to a course of destruction. America had once manifested a unity of purpose around unselfish goals such as the defeat of Nazi Germany and of Imperial Japan. Who could ever dissent from such noble enterprises? The war was followed by a period of consolidation around the idea that America was the bulwark of freedom and democracy. The Alliance for Progress and the Peace Corps helped to undo any thought that victorious America would use its power to advance the old colonial rule.

There followed the domestic liberation era of the freedom riders and of the Student Non-violent Coordinating Committee to advance desegregation and the various liberation movements for women and for homosexuals. The presumption that was most prevalent as the century came to an end without a nuclear conflict was that victory had been achieved and a new era had dawned at last. It had come as a great surprise then when in the wake of the terrorist incidents of 2003 the subsequent elective wars of George W. Bush and company took over a trillion dollars out of American hands to support a new colonialism.

This in turn was followed by the Great Recession of 2008 that brought the realization that far from being delivered from the ills bred of past evils the 21st century would likely bring about unprecedented challenges to our collective planetary survival let alone question American supremacy. It was this realization that had provided the backdrop of the education of young Abraham Cardozo and he reacted to it by embracing the solutions offered by the Progressive Democrats as opposed to the equally strident call of conservative Republicans for a return to a version of America that had ceased with the publication of *The Saturday Evening Post* and *Life Magazine*. All that remained of the old journalism was represented by survivors such as: *The New Yorker, Atlantic Monthly*, and the twin publications *Time* and *Newsweek*. For more specialized audiences there was: *The Economist, Mother*

Jones, America, Commonweal, or *Rolling Stone.*

But even these could not supply the unified consensus of the no longer existing mainstream American consciousness. Instead there was only the nightly vituperation of the feuds between Fox News and CNN. It was the age of contention and vituperation. He thought of the bile spewing forth from pretty faces. He thought of the almost monthly stories of shootings in schools and workplaces. Still the Republican dike held firm, the Second Amendment and the refusal of service to homosexuals must stay firm; guns God and glory were the American motto. For Abraham detachment meant to get beyond all of this in order to recover what had once been the collective peace of mind that had once enabled Americans to pursue collective goals simply as Americans.

Abraham was young. It takes confidence to make commitments to a way of life. It takes a sense that the future is at least marginally predictable in its general trends. Absent this inner sense of stability it is natural to abjure commitments and to refuse to invest the scarce and irreplaceable capital of one's youth in any sustained project. Even to have attended law school may have been ill-advised, he reflected, considering the supply of young attorneys and the shrinking availability of clients who are both able and willing to hire private outside counsel to solve their legal problems.

But where besides the law could a young reformer look to combine a sense of mission with expertise in the mindless but automated rush of events? Abraham felt doomed to the institution of the law, set aside by the same impetuous impulse and colloquy with the divine that had led to the founding of Israel. He had awoken one day to the fact that he possessed a world conscience, one that demanded that he address various ills over which he had neither influence nor control. It was an attitude that when less politically grounded and more a result of metaphysical melancholy had been called by the German term, Weltschmerz. This was the pain that accompanied our young hero each season as he set off into the desert of sand and sea on the coast to seek an answer to his ever receding question: what is the meaning of it all and where do I fit in.

The following day he awoke to a day of high clouds and wind. It was time to move southwards so he checked out of his room in Lincoln City and moved south to Yachats, a town of retired academic types and artists just north of Florence and the Oregon Dunes.

Yachats is the perfect place to seek the serenity of reminiscence while looking out from the cliffs to the never changing panorama of rock and sea. It is rather like the early Carmel of Jack London and of Robinson Jeffers, a place of retreat and individuality for people who know that nothing good can ever come out of a faculty meeting. Comfortable but unpretentious its natives divide the day into the quadrants of early morning coffee, afternoon tea, sunset, and sleep. They enjoy the lassitude of enlightened discussion without the obligation to leave serenity behind and to plunge back into the fray. Yachats is a good place to recuperate after victory over a protracted illness or to forget an unseasonable love affair. To Abraham it was only a wayside in his endless quest for beatitude.

Beatitude, that was the actual origin of the term "beat" as in "beatniks," the band of young writers in the 1950's who sought redemption and ecstasy in New York City and along America's highways. These were the true believers in that absurd and antiquated term, the American Dream. Instead, what most of American literature does with the term is to chronicle the American disappointment instead.

One need only read such works as *The Education of Henry Adams, Pierre, The Marble Faun, The Grapes of Wrath, Day of the Locust,* or *The Great Gatsby* to prove this point. America is all too often the story of betrayed innocence. It is the same drama that was being enacted daily on our southern border with Mexico. America combines opportunity with moral entropy in a way that is distinctively American. It was just as Arthur Miller noted in his great play, *Death of a Salesman*: the ones who are most lethally wounded are the true-believers. America lacks the comforting cynicism of the French and the long adaptation to suffering of the Russians. This makes our literature the perfect candidate for tragedy, the ruin of one who once had such great expectations.

Abraham had no desire to court disappointment by engaging, by joining in the final orgiastic feast. For this reason he had early on elected to pursue a policy of selective disillusionment to serve as an inoculation against the illness of despair. He sought the sub-text to every claim of easy redemption. He realized that the Promised Land was always just over the horizon and at least one generation distant. His abiding sense was that enough would be provided to fill his momentary needs but no more. To aspire to more was both unnecessary and foolish; therefore he detached himself from any attitude of expectation beyond that of simply awaiting the logical resolution of social forces. Yet, in spite of this conscious policy he felt driven to embrace a reformist agenda as applied to those general social trends that transcend any individual decision. The worst disasters of humankind were not matters of deliberate policy it seemed but rather spontaneous eruptions of disaster from the elusive threads of minor causality. Insofar as he possessed heroic faith it was not based upon any creed or singular proposition but rather stemmed from his refusal to accept the opposite, that this world is inherently flawed, the off-scouring of a better universe by the demiurge. While not a formal stoic he was more apt to adopt a bitter frown and a stiff upper lip than tears in the face of misfortune. If he was prone to any lasting weakness it was irritation that corrections did not produce immediate and salutary results. Life simply continued and one must make do as best one could. That was then; this was now. There was no more to be said.

He did not assume that an overarching deity micromanaged events nor could he accept a negligent deity that by shifting its attention elsewhere simply overlooked noxious or terrible agents until they had done their nefarious work upon prostrate humankind. If he had been Christian rather than Jewish he might have found comfort in the cross. Instead there was only the comfort of the Torah as the best devotional path for life to follow and the assurance that behind the many distinctions of the Talmud there was an abiding and comforting presence the nature of which could never be expressed directly but only indicated by that name that could never be uttered.

Upon arriving in Yachats Abraham left his car in the parking lot and opened the driftwood studded door where he confirmed his reservation at the front desk for the next several days while he explored Yachats and its environs. His room was on the ground floor with ready access to the winding shore path along the tidal pools. He deposited his luggage and lay down fully clothed on the bed. Outside the sound of the surf was gentle and soothing. Already the journey seemed distant and dreamlike to him as though he had always found here his restful abode and place of solace.

Was this what detachment meant? To be in a place where all that mattered was a sufficient credit or debit card balance? As he drifted off to sleep Abraham imagined an endless series of just such picturesque and remote establishments designed to enhance the comforts of their guests. Was travel the final achievement of civilization? In that case of what possible use or necessity could there be for any particular promised land? Were these concepts anything beyond a justification for various nationalisms or ethnic expansions? Was the idea of a greater Serbia anything beyond a Balkan version of the old American doctrine of Manifest Destiny? For the eternal wanderer no home is needed or even requested. A traveler is never a refugee because he seeks no other refuge than the fastest way out of town, his only goal the distant horizon. To stand still is to allow the tendrils of routine to entwine their choking grip and with long acquaintance comes insolence and contempt.

When he awoke it was time for a quick shower followed by dinner. He was near enough to walk to a restaurant that he recalled from prior years where he ordered a Pimm's Cup to drink and a salmon filet seasoned with tarragon. The high tide of evening was running into the cove and the sea had that silver sheen that betokens a clear view of the coming sunset. He felt relaxed but not lethargic and the crisp icy taste of his cocktail brought his appetite to a razor's keenness. The big world seemed very distant here. The various struggles, migrations, threats and counter-threats; what were these to this narrow band of pearl-like hamlets strung along the great green plain of ocean. Time slowed here. It seemed as though he had traversed a great expanse already since dawn, not of space but of existence and its accompanist, perception.

"Why do I ever leave here?" he thought to himself.

But there is always the need to get more money, to retain one's job or to maintain one's business and all the while our constituent cells age and the threat of incipient mutiny lies harbored within our tissues. We imagine an accounting of time that is self-replenishing so that every withdrawal will be recouped by an equal margin of interest on our investment. Each promotion brings the life of permanent vacation and retirement closer. The plums of affluence grow riper on the tree. But suddenly we realize that by harvest time we may have forgotten or lost in some obscure manner that electric excitement that once gave a point to everything. Joy cannot be summoned up at will. When we lose scarcity we lose meaning. There is a mocking law of diminishing returns at the point where we can afford the preconditions of security. For this reason we should allow nothing to escape us. Walter Pater was right in his description of the transient nature of all things and the need to pay attention to life's incipient seasons.

Suddenly his dinner was before him, piquant and redolent of the local waters. He ate with contentment, savoring each buttery morsel. The sun sank slowly lower and by the time his coffee and dessert was served the day was perceptibly cooler and the outer doors were shut. He was happy to have brought a sweater with him from his room. The wind often rose just before sunset. A sense of quiet awe sets in; the world comes alive as though protesting even this minor death although tomorrow the same pageant will be repeated as it always has been. Abraham felt though that with each sunset there should be enacted some appropriate ritual to ensure the sun's return. Even minor partings bring their weight of sadness.

He arose and paid his bill before exiting to the sea path. Great plumbs of spray arose as the breakers thundered into the narrow chasms that could not accommodate their impetuous onrush. The sun sank lower and lower and even the mists on the horizon seemed to melt and give way before it. At last the whole sea seemed to catch fire and the distant clouds to glow with yellow or orange reflections.

A silence descended upon the people walking slowly along the path with him. A sort of community of matched thoughts possessed them all and the sun began to burn its way into the sea. A short six minutes later the contracting disk was no more, its light only an upward projection from where it now reclined beneath the horizon. The wind was more intense now and a chill grew gradually on the driftwood studded sands by the river. Abraham watched as the little groups passed him with a nod or a complicit smile as though all and each were sharers in a vast conspiracy born of witnessing this universal event.

A short time later he had returned to his room. He took out the third volume of Sir Osbert Sitwell's autobiography, read for an hour, and then fell asleep to the slow pounding music of the sea.

The next day Abraham had planned on visiting the northernmost reaches of the Oregon Dunes lying just over the bridge from Florence. He decided to retain his room in Yachats to return to that night. A quick breakfast of an orange butter-horn and coffee sufficed for breakfast and he set out to see the nearby sights.

He paid the entrance fee and climbed the winding road to the top of Cape Perpetua just south of town. From its summit a vast panorama of rock and chasm is visible and the sea seems to climb until it lies within a few centimeters of one's eyes gazing outwards, a great bank of blueness that might at any moment overflow and falling inwards lap about one's feet. He sat in the long grass with his back against a stone to savor infinity. He recalled the German students he had met up here once in days gone by. They had all exchanged addresses and promised to write in order to preserve the remnants of an instant friendship but had never done so. Or was it he who had failed to respond? How many open invitations do we pass up simply through neglect?

Abraham wondered at the number of strands of parallel lives that died of just such negligence and attrition. It made him think that no one is really a stranger. If time allowed it should be possible to reach a lover's depth with all the world. He wondered if there was such a thing as an omni-sexual, not in the genital sense, but in the sense that one quivered to the passing embrace of eyes on a subway platform or a smile that might have been only courtesy but in its completeness managed to sum up a lifetime of foregone acquaintance and intimacy.

His namesake, Justice Benjamin Cardozo, had never married—for him there was only the infinite play of the great man's mind and the all sufficient power of words. While for the great patriarch of old, Father Abraham, there was his wife Sara and the servant girl Hagar. From his loins came the people Israel and the long history of suffering and exile that was the greater part of Jewish history. What could he learn from these men regarding what changes and what might just possibly abide? Would our young hero ever marry or father forth offspring to be cast adrift on the surging waters of the 21st century? This brief narrative must be all encompassing and his life trail off into that infinite regress implied in the word "maybe." He liked to consider himself a procreative optimist. In spite of the challenges the human race must soon endure it would be a false prudence to fail to procreate out of fear that human beings are not up to any challenge, even the wasting of the planet itself. There must be someone left to bear witness even to cosmic ruin and to write a final codicil to the last will and testament of humanity.

With this vow in his heart Abraham descended to the ribbon of highway below and turned south towards Neptune Beach and Strawberry Hill. From there he turned the tight corner of road at Heceta Head and climbed to the access point to the Sea Lion Caves. He pulled off the road at the top of the cliffs and got out of his car to look back on the Heceta Head Lighthouse where it lay tucked just behind the Devil's Elbow with its white encrustations of guano from the various seabirds.

The great foaming waves at the base of the cliffs revealed great colonies of brown sea lions. Flocks of hovering seagulls surfed in the sky over the abyss. It was an awesome place of land and ocean: remote, adamantine, and primeval. He remained there poised on the balance-point of wonder yet summoned again to resume his journey by the insistent tug of his outlined plans for the day. The next stop was to be Florence-by-the-Sea. Had he attended law school in Eugene rather than in Washington this town would have associations different from those that had actually prevailed. Eight law schools had accepted him, each boding a different subsequent fate. Had he chosen correctly? How could he ever know? Who can bear up under the awesome chains of contingency that life imposes? But he was here now and in that "nowness" resides our only true freedom.

Florence lies along the Siuslaw River where it meets the sea. He stopped there before proceeding across the bridge to the dunes overlook for a bowl of clam chowder, a mild violation of kosher prohibition. He would make it up later by a prayer intoned over the sand dunes, blessing all that is. He was sure that the Baal Shem Tov would understand.

Abraham's relation to his faith was hereditary and tangential rather than strictly observant. He valued the essential virtues that had emerged among his co-religionists over centuries of historic marginalization. Not least among these were the sayings of the Hasidic Rabbis. It seemed obvious to Abraham that the best way to resolve the endless religious contentions that were dividing the world would to be for God to call a general colloquy of representatives from the major monotheistic religions together, have everyone bring their favorite proof texts along in little binders, and proceed to show them in detail how historical drift and animosities had blurred the essentials in an ever-growing mound of miniscule accretions.

It seemed to be an insuperable task to sift through all the claims and counter-claims of religious discourse to discover the original bond between God and humanity. The beginnings are shrouded in the dense fog of illiteracy or else the records were simply misfiled or destroyed. It was pointless to apply the metaphysical equivalent of the Best Evidence Rule and to request an original rather than a copy. Councils, synods, schools, commentaries, speculations, original sects, revelations, prophesies, mystical visions, ecstasies: all had restated and amended that first encounter where the Celestial Presence addressed the two dripping bipeds with loins still wet due to the mindless mandate of copulation and enjoined the first codified rules of human conduct. Perhaps the most salient characteristic of the 21st century was not the threat of technology and artificial intelligence after all: the major wars would likely be over a zero-sum struggle over competing revelations and contrasting versions of metaphysics.

After a late lunch Abraham left Old Town behind and with a pocket full of salt-water taffy got back on the highway, crossed the bridge at the far end of town, and headed for the dune overlook exit. After leaving the highway a cut-off to the left beckoned and he found a parking lot where various trucks were unloading dune buggies to join the many noisy vehicles that were engaged in climbing a seventy foot mound of sand before him. The top was invisible but a path to the right through the evergreen trees beckoned and Abraham began to climb.

He found that others had been there before him and by placing his feet carefully in their footsteps he could minimize the soft subsiding avalanche as he asked the sand to support his weight. By means of this strategy he managed to climb to a fairly level surface at the crest of the great dune. From this vantage point a marvelous sight emerged. There before him lay a virtual desert as of fabled Arabia, dune after dune only interrupted by small copses of evergreen trees like sheltered isles of repose in a fawn colored sea. The great expanse of sand dunes fell off westward in steep cliffs and a mile distant the ocean appeared beyond the lower moonscape of sea grass and beach blue and infinite. Abraham climbed higher still towards where the cliffs began and sat down on a fallen and bleached out pine tree to catch his breath again after his long climb. Here he was almost beyond the roar of the dune buggies and something of the primal aspect of the scene was restored. Isolation returned and with it the luxury of thought.

He returned to his speculations upon time and history. He thought of the great disproportion between texts and actuality. If God were to write anything down then surely His text must be creation itself existing above any interpretation. It seemed strange to him therefore that the great religions seemed to emphasize the jurisprudential aspect of the Divine Intellect rather than simply to contemplate the wonder of being. The emphasis upon the will of God seemed secondary to a contemplation and appreciation of what God had already accomplished.

Abraham was neither a pantheist nor a disciple of Spinoza but he did feel that commandments had more to do with human needs than with divine mandates. Morality appeared to him to reside at the metaphysical level of parking regulations. The oscillating rhythm of sin and forgiveness, of mercy or retribution, of command and acquiescence seemed to be too infused by the human element to really matter, at least from the distant perspective of the philosopher. But on the other hand, who could quarrel with revelation provided that that revelation was authentic and not biased in some manner by the one who initially recorded it? To understand the intricacies of Divine Inspiration though was beyond the present ambit of the time and place of Abraham's speculations.

But as a bare proposition subject to correction: assuming that the reflection of God's essence lay within his creation, it showed a variety and even a quality of spontaneity that was alien to most supposedly definitive summations and interpretations by the major religions. It seemed to Abraham that closure was one of the last attributes to be implied in regard to the Godhead. All of the huffing and puffing of various imams, clerics, and avatars of the sublime to ensure that God not be offended seemed to forget the sheer silent witness of being in places like this, holding the slow accretion of eons of wind, sand, and season. Humankind lies awash in conflicting mandates and proposed punishments so that the justice and majesty of God might be vindicated at last.

Abraham thought about it all. Could God do nothing for Himself but he must rely upon various factions of our fellow men to threaten us into compliance? He thought of his proposed manuscript at home and wondered whether what so many of his conservative countrymen were calling for was a theistic version of the absurd red hats that appeared at various Trump rallies proclaiming that America could be great again; God could be great again as long as we make it happen.

Was it an accident that political fundamentalists were usually religious fundamentalists as well? What a shock it must be for those who believe that they can speak authoritatively for God himself to discover that they are powerless beyond the grim circle of their own rhetoric. How frustrating it must be to recall the days when they could call forth armies and wade through seas of blood to impose their doctrines and covenants. Now they were reduced to mere frothing diatribes and appeals for sacrifice on the part of the faithful to advance their particular crusade, jihad, or ministry.

In America there was the great alliance of the born subjugators of others whose uncertainty demanded compliance as the proof that they had been right all along in the cosmic sweepstakes. All of history was a reflection of how they had used their power when they still possessed it.

    Suddenly Abraham saw what was really happening in this critical hour of history. For the first time all contending absolutes were stripped down and lined up on an equal starting line on the final sprint to the finish, winner take all. There they stood with sinews lithe and straining, great chests heaving with maledictions towards the heretics and false witnesses lined up next to them in competition. Each contender pointed at the skies where ranks of serried angels awaited the outcome, fearsome and furious but determined to let some inscrutable inward certification be rewarded by victory while all others must watch as their laurels turned to chains dragging them into a pit of more than defeat, a pit of utter punishment, shame, and desolation. Victory! A blare of trumpets, the great city arises…

Abraham Cardozo awoke to the sound of the wind blowing through the trees above his head. It was late. He would obtain no more food tonight. The stars already floated in the clear sky of night, silent and remote. Restaurants close early on the Oregon coast. He might just stop for some kippers at a grocery store before heading back to his room in Yachats.

    He retraced his thoughts assembled like grains of sand in the face of this great immensity. If he had possessed a papyrus roll he might have recorded his thoughts even as St. John had done in exile on the remote island of Patmos. He could slip the manuscript into a vessel or tie it with a ribbon only to have it be discovered years later like the scrolls of Nag Hammadi. Scholars would puzzle over the mysterious author and the size of the community of followers that he must have gathered about him.

    Alas the city that they had envisioned had long since crumbled into sand and all that remained was this sacred testimony as witness to the vision vouchsafed so long ago. Abraham thought of the new versions of Mishnah and Gemara that might ensue from his simple act of climbing the dune alone on a summer day. He bethought him of the various schools of thought, the carefully calibrated distinctions, the condemnations and excommunications, the many dying in anguish still unsure of their salvation, lamenting their sins but secretly knowing in their heart of hearts that granted youth and time enough they might commit them again, not to offend God, but simply because they were human, overwhelmed by the passions and uncertainties spared to those who parsing sacred texts knew better, or feared more, or simply had a professional interest in being right. Perhaps they were. Who was he to say?

    He took his notebook from his pocket and stood there, ball-point pen in hand. What was his vision? Abraham looked about him at the moonlit sea, the sand, and the beacons of starlight as the darkness deepened. He listened to the wind sighing in the long sea-grass. The granular presence of this little slice of eternity blew softly about his sandaled feet and he who might have been the great law-giver and father of nations put aside his writing implements, trudged wearily back down over the sifting dunes and drove quietly away.

UNHAPPY ENDINGS
BY CARRIE AVERY MORIARTY

Content Warning: This story deals with mental health issues and suicide.

"What do you mean it's not here?" Shelly asked.

"Just what I said," Richard replied. "It's not here."

"Did you look?"

Richard looked at her, eyebrows raised. "No," he barked. "I walked in, and when it didn't jump into my hands, I had to assume it wasn't here."

The sarcasm in his voice set her off.

"Never mind," she muttered. "I'll look myself."

"Why do you never believe me?"

Not answering, Shelly began moving papers and folders around the desk, looking in each one. After her thorough search, she concluded, "It's not here."

"Just like I told you," Richard said.

"So," she began. "Where is it?"

"I think I would have it in my hands if I knew that," he said.

"Where did you have it last?"

"At my desk," he said. "Which is why I was looking for it there. I wonder if Karen picked it up and filed it."

"Why would she file it?"

"Because it's her job," Richard said walking out the door.

"It's her job to take things from your desk and file them?" Shelly asked, following him out the door.

"Karen," Richard said as he got to her desk.

"What can I do for you, boss?"

"Have you seen the Mackenzie documents?"

"They were on your desk this morning," she replied. "I knew you were working on that project today, so I left them there."

"Well," Shelly said. "They seem to have grown legs and wandered off."

"Oh dear," Karen replied. "Let me check with Mark."

Picking up the receiver on her phone, she pressed a couple of buttons, then waited.

"Yeah," she said into the receiver. "Have you seen Mackenzie?" She paused, then asked, "Can you check your desk?" Another pause. "I'll wait." Placing her hand over the mouthpiece she said, "He's checking his desk."

"Obviously," Shelly muttered.

Richard gave her a glare, then patiently waited for the answer.

"Great," Karen said. "Bring it on up."

"Why did he have it?" Shelly asked once the phone was back on its cradle.

"We can ask him when he gets here," Karen responded.

"We'll be in my office," Richard replied, gripping his sister's arm and nearly dragging her into the office, closing the door behind them.

"Why aren't you waiting out there?" she barked. "Don't your employees know to leave things where they are?"

"Shelly," Richard said sternly. "I trust my employees. They were hired because of their professionalism and work ethic. I do not need you coming in here and thinking you can read them the riot act because you perceive some kind of injustice."

"I never," she sputtered.

"Exactly," he responded. "This is why the firm was left to me, not you. I have the business degree. I have the smarts to run the company the way Dad and Granddad wanted it run. It is my responsibility to make sure that things run smoothly for everyone, clients and employees alike. Until the board sees fit to remove me from my position, you need to trust that I know what is best and that I will work to make sure that things run smoothly."

"Why are you so bossy?"

"I'm not bossy," he corrected. "I am firm with my convictions, something Dad couldn't bring himself to be where you were concerned. He always let you get away with things you shouldn't have, and it's left you with less coping skills and not nearly enough common sense as you should have by this age."

"Seriously, Richard," she tried. "Why can't you just let me be part of the company? It's my legacy just as much as it is yours."

"And I'll make sure the legacy is still around," he said.

Just then, a knock sounded on his door. Opening it, he saw Karen, Mackenzie file in hand.

"Here you go, boss," she said.

"Thank you, Karen," he said. "And thank Mark, too."

Everyone at the firm knew that Shelly Draper was not in charge, even though she liked to throw her name around to get attention. Newer employees were warned that she was to be respected, but anything she demanded needed to be run by her brother prior to any work actually being done on the project.

"My pleasure," she replied, closing the door.

"Let me have it," Shelly said, reaching for the file.

"Sit," Richard barked.

"I'm not a dog," Shelly retorted.

"No," Richard said. "They are much better behaved than you. Now sit and we'll talk about it."

"Sometimes I just hate you," she mumbled, but complied with her brother's wish and sat in one of the chairs next to his desk.

Walking behind the desk, he sat, opening the file on top of the stack of others that were there. Shelly bounced in her seat, impatience obvious in her demeanor.

"Looks like Mark was doing the work I planned to get to after lunch today," he said.

"Why is he doing it when it isn't his job?"

"It actually is his job," Richard said. "Sometimes, however, I pick up any slack that might happen because of someone else's work load. This was one of those times. Turned out he didn't need my help after all."

"So," she hedged, leaning forward. "What is happening?"

Richard held up his finger as he reviewed the top page in the file. He then clicked on his keyboard a few times to pull up the electronic file. A few mouse clicks later he turned to his sister.

"We got it," he said.

"Yeah," she shouted, jumping from her chair. "I'm so excited. When do I get to hold it?"

"Shelly," he said sternly. "Sit."

"Still not a dog," she replied, but complied again with his instructions.

"While we have claimed the art," he began, "it doesn't mean we'll have it here tomorrow. It takes time for these things to go through the proper channels. It has to be brought to the country, make it through customs, be authenticated, and after all of that is done, then it will be shipped to the warehouse. Once it's there, a final inspection will be done. After that, it will be available for us to display it as we have already discussed. You are not going to get to hold it."

"It's a stupid vase," she gruffed. "Why can't we just have it at the house?"

"Because it is worth half a million dollars," Richard replied.

"So," Shelly said.

"So," he replied. "It will be kept in a safe place where it will not come to any harm. This vase is several hundred years old. It's not like one you can buy on a shelf at some store. It's a treasure that needs to be properly displayed."

"But it's pretty," she complained. "And I want to be able to look at it any time I'm sad. It cheers me up."

"You're just going to have to find something a little less expensive to do that," he said.

"Are you going to commission replicas to sell?"

"We just got the go ahead to make the purchase," he said. "I haven't had a chance to discuss anything with my team. Until that happens, no decisions can be made."

"I think you should make sure there are replicas," she said. "Then, anyone who is sad can buy one and have it at their home to make them happy."

"I'll take that request under advisement," he said. "Now, can I get back to my actual job? There are other things that I need to take care of."

"OK," she replied. "See you when you get home."

She walked out the door, leaving it open on her exit. Richard sighed once he knew she was well out of earshot. He loved his sister dearly, but she was such a high maintenance person he couldn't handle being around her for long periods of time. Karen walked in a few minutes after Shelly left, closing the door behind her.

"You are a saint," she said. "I don't know how you deal with her on a daily basis. She is exhausting."

"Hey," he replied.

"I know," she said. "She's family, so you just have to put up with it."

"Thank you for running the file down," he said.

"It's my job," she replied. "So?"

"We got it," he smiled. "Now I just have to get through all the hoops to get it here. She wants replicas to be available."

"You told her you can't do that, right?"

"I told her I'd check with my team," he replied.

"But, Richard," Karen said.

"I know," he replied. "I just had to get her out of here. Even I have my limits as to how much I can take of her. She would have probably gone into full meltdown mode if I'd told her no."

"As long as you don't make me tell her," Karen replied.

"I'll tell her something," he said.

"Mark said he'd be ready whenever you were done," she said.

"I'll head down there now," he replied.

"Hey," Richard said at Mark's doorway.

Mark looked up from his computer and pushed his glasses up on top of his head.

"You alone?" he whispered.

"Yeah," Richard said as he came into the room. "She left after I told her we got it."

"I don't know how you do it," Mark said.

"What?"

"Put up with her crazy," Mark replied.

"I guess I'm just used to it," Richard said.

"I don't think I could ever get used to that," Mark laughed.

"What are our next steps?" Richard asked, steering the conversation back to business.

"The letters are ready for your approval," Mark replied. "Once you've reviewed them, I'll get them printed and sent out. Should only take a week or so to get the answers we need. After that, it's just a matter of waiting on the government. We all know how quickly they move on these types of things."

"Yes," Richard replied. "What's your next project?"

"This was the last one," Mark said.

"What do you mean?"

"You remember I'm moving, right?"

"Oh, yeah," Richard said. "I completely forgot about that. Where are you going, again?"

"I'm going back to Montana," Mark replied. "Dad isn't doing well, and mom wants me to come home and take over the business for him."

"You will be sorely missed," Richard remarked. "But I really do wish you well on this new chapter."

"Thanks," Mark replied.

"I'll let you get back to it," Richard said, walking out the door.

"Shelly called," Karen said as Richard made it back to his office.

"She just left," Richard said.

"Oh, I know," Karen said.

"What did she want?"

"Apparently she wants to go to Brazil and look at something someone discovered down there," Karen said without expression.

Richard sighed, running a hand across his face. "Why does she do this to me?"

"You're asking the wrong person," Karen replied.

"I don't think anyone has the answer," Richard said, then stepped into his office.

Sitting at his desk, he pulled up his sister's favorite website for searches on new finds in Brazil. At the top of the list was a portion of an urn. The notes indicated that it was from far before the Portuguese came to the country, but it couldn't be confirmed at this point. Of course his sister would want to get that. She was all about things that predated the western influence in South America, and this was no different.

His phone buzzed and he picked up the handset. "Yes," he said.

"She's on line one," Karen said.

"I'll take it," he replied, then pressed the button for the line. "Hello, Shelly," he said.

"Did Karen tell you I called?"

"Yes," he replied. "I am looking at what I think you are interested in."

"The urn?" she asked.

"That's what I figured," he sighed.

"It could hold the key," she bubbled.

"Or it could just be another thing you set your mind on," he said.

"Can I go?"

"Are you seriously asking me this?"

"I want to go," she begged.

"You know I can't let you," he argued.

"But it could be exactly what I need," she replied.

"Until I see more information on it," he began, "I'm not going to put any time into it."

"I'll do it all," she offered.

"You can't," he replied.

"Why?" she asked. "Because I'm too dumb? Or because I'm crazy?"

"Shelly," Richard sighed. "We have been over this with every piece you've found. I can't allow you to travel alone, and I can't afford to have a team go with you. We will have to wait and see what new information they come up with before we make any plans as to whether or not to get it."

"It's the key," she demanded. "I can feel it in my soul."

"Shelly," he barked. "Just stop. I have a business to run, and that requires all of my time. I cannot give you any more time to follow these foolish notions you have of finding a cure. You need to learn to live with it."

"You just don't understand," she shouted back. "You don't have to live like I do. No one tells you when to get up or when to go to bed. They don't make you take stupid pills every day that do nothing but drown your creativity. I can't even decide what I want to eat because of it. I want freedom. I want to really live. And you're just determined to keep me locked up. I bet if you could get away with it, you would lock me in a dungeon and throw away the key. You'd leave me to rot in the dark."

Richard pinched the bridge of his nose, trying to hold back his anger.

"Shelly," he began. "I love you. You're my sister. You are the only part of my family that's left. I know you don't mean to be horrible, but you need to understand that everything I do is for your own good."

"You hate me," she shouted, then disconnected the call.

Sighing, he placed the receiver back in its cradle. "That woman is going to be the death of me," he muttered.

"I'm home," Richard called as he came into the house.

The silence around him was deafening.

"Hello?" he called.

Still nothing.

He placed his briefcase on the credenza in the entry and made his way to the kitchen. Surely someone was here. Usually he could smell dinner when he walked in, but the house felt cold and empty as he made his way through it.

Stepping into the kitchen he grabbed his stomach, one hand going over his mouth. Nothing prepared him for the sight he was met with. On the floor was their cook, Julia. Her throat was slit all the way across, blood pooling around her head. Her eyes stared in horror at the ceiling. Next to her was Gloria, the housekeeper. She was in the same state, throat sliced all the way across, a puddle of blood under her as well.

"Shelly," he shouted, racing from the room and back the way he came. He took the steps to the second level two at a time, bounding up the stairs as fast as he could. Racing down the hall, he ripped open his sister's door and stopped cold.

"Oh, Shelly," he sobbed as he saw her on the bed.

Stepping up next to it, he looked down into the peaceful face of his sister. If he didn't know better, he'd think she was just resting. But her eyes were wide, her lips blue, and a faint trace of blood had dribbled from the corner of her mouth. In her hand she held an empty pill bottle. He picked it up and turned the bottle, reading the label.

On the night stand he saw a nearly empty bottle of whiskey and a bloody butcher knife. He closed his eyes, swallowing back the bile that rose in his throat. He placed the pill bottle next to the whiskey, turned, and left the room.

"I understand this must be difficult for you," the detective said.

"I just can't believe she did all of this," Richard replied.

It hadn't taken long for the police to arrive after he'd made the call. First to arrive were uniformed officers, followed by detectives, and finally the county coroner. He'd explained the situation when he'd called 911, telling the agent that no one would be able to be saved. He'd told the story so many times he'd lost count.

"It seems like she was having some issues," the detective offered.

"She's mentally unstable," Richard replied.

"Was she on any other medication?"

"I've got a list of her medications in the book," he said. "She had more than mental health issues. There were also physical issues she had going on."

"If you can get me a list of her doctors," the detective began.

"I have a notebook that has all of the information in it," Richard said. "It has her providers, list of medications, last visit notes, and everything about her conditions."

"What conditions did she have?"

"She contracted polio when she was a child," Richard explained.

"Didn't she get vaccinated?"

"Unfortunately, her body had a tendency to refuse vaccines," Richard began. "She could get the dosage and within a week, no trace of it would be found in her system. We went to Nigeria on a safari when we were little and she contracted it there."

"I didn't even think it was around anymore," the detective said.

"It's pretty much gone," Richard replied. "There are very few places where it is still around, and we happened to go to one of them."

"You said she had mental health issues," the officer suggested.

"She was schizophrenic," Richard said. "She was on medication for it, but her dosage had recently changed. It's in the book."

"Can you get the book?"

"Sure." Richard stood and walked to his office. Reaching up onto the shelf, he pulled down the black notebook where all of Shelly's medical information was kept. He turned and handed it to the officer.

"Do you mind if we hold onto this for a while?"

"That's fine," Richard said.

"I think this is all I need for now," the detective said. "Here's my card, if you think of anything else."

"Thank you," he replied. "I know this can't be easy for you, either."

"Death is never easy," the detective said. "Whether it's for the family or for those who have to investigate it."

"I appreciate you're being so kind," Richard said.

"We'll be in touch," the detective said, then walked out of the office.

Richard could still hear the rest of the authorities mulling around the house, finishing up their tasks. When someone knocked on the office door, he raised his eyes to look at the man.

"We're all done," he said. "Once the coroner has completed the autopsies, you will be informed of the results."

"Thank you," Richard replied.

"I'm sorry for your loss," the man said, then turned and left.

Richard heard the front door close, then held his breath, listening to the lack of sound. Breathing out heavily, he stood from the desk to assess what was left to accomplish. He did not relish the cleanup that awaited him.

Three days later.

"I'm so sorry for your loss," the man said.

It was the hundredth time Richard had heard the phrase that day. But it was to be expected. He'd opted to have the funeral open to the public, and apparently Shelly had quite a few friends around town. Hundreds had come out for the service, and they were all filing out now. Soon, he would be left without any distractions.

"How are you holding up?" Karen asked.

"I'll survive," he replied.

"If you need anything," she said.

"Thanks," he responded.

The two women his sister had killed had been buried at their family's request, and Richard had paid for everything, including a generous severance package that did nothing to ease his guilt over their deaths. What he wanted to do was rewind time and see the warning signs that must have been there. He should have known his sister was dangerous, should have been able to prevent the tragedy. But that wasn't something he could control.

He'd decided to have the open ceremony at the funeral home, but had not invited anyone to the burial at the cemetery. That, he wanted to do on his own. Once he made it there, he climbed from his car and walked to the open grave. His sister's body had arrived and was placed in the contraption that would lower her into the ground.

"Why did you do it?" he asked the box.

Of course he didn't get a response. He was left with only questions and no answers. He would never know the reasoning behind what his sister had done. The coroner had confirmed that she'd overdosed on the medication shortly after the other women had been killed. They had been struck on the head, then their throats had been cut while they were unconscious. It was swift and seemingly painless for them, mercifully.

Shelly hadn't suffered, either. She'd taken several of the pills, combined with the whisky she'd used to swallow them, and had simply fallen asleep and never woke up. They had determined it happened shortly after she got home from her trip to his office that morning, just after the phone call in which she accused him of not caring about her. Nothing could have saved any of the women, and Richard had to simply live with that fact.

THE PROCESS
BY DAVID MECKLENBURG

Compulsion and habit move together. They clasp each other's hand, just as they did in the womb, each so intimate with the other that the outside world cannot differentiate them. I don't dress them up in the same clothes, although they often make that decision on their own. They stir beneath the comforter before I am awake, hatching out the plans and intrigues which are always the same. They dispense with preliminaries; I get into the shower, I soap up, I rinse, I wash my hair and if it's Wednesday they allow me the novelty of shampooing it. A deeper rhythm suggests masturbation with the shower massager on certain days and it is a time where I am allowed a bit of freedom with whichever phantom I choose to make love. Thursdays I shave my legs and upper lip.

    The completion of my toilet: the towel wrapped around my

head, and a robe on (if it's cold). I warm up the coffee I made in ritualistic abasement the night before. With a black cup of life, I return to the bathroom to pull out the random hairs that mark age, hoping the violent extirpation will render the follicles barren and lifeless. I moisturize and scent myself and then tend to the tangle of my hair. I choose my clothes. If it is a skirt, I often put my shoes on first. I'm not sure why, but I have always done this save when I lived in Japan for six months. Exercise? That waits for the evening, so its place is not here. I eat, or rather drink my breakfast. A bit of lipstick and I am off.

    I am compressing time at the end. This is usually because I am in a hurry. The habit of leisure has encroached a bit on the compulsion to go to work. To earn my money. To sit or stand at my desk and type other people's words. I am typing these words which are mine, but I somehow forgot that we share these words—in this order, this context of habit: this compulsion of moving from left to right with our gaze—we would not understand one another where it otherwise. Are these my words?

    I write these words on a ferryboat. I am commuting. I wonder if the tense is correct, to switch between present, present perfect, past. The subjunctive, long forgotten by many who speak and write English, always lurks, waits, ready to spring up were it given the chance. Ada writes mostly in first person; it feels comfortable, fresh and immediate, although the extra-egotistical perspective of third person always brings fresh insights. The second person promises similar interest: a similar vantage point but like standing in a line it becomes tedious. You understand.

    Physically, I need a little variance. This floating room of my own is not my own; it is public. Hundreds of other people are on board, but such is the culture I live in that we sequester. A few are social in the same seats they always occupy. Most sleep or lose themselves in their mobile devices. A few read books. I like them the best. Some work. A cadre of coders constantly type on laptops. Others make deals on phones. A few people text. I write. This.

Whim barges in on the Syzygy of compulsion and habit.

—what is it going to be today? Pen, keyboard? The big journal? Quotes or Joycean dashes?

"I'm not really sure, but I feel like a keyboard today."

—Volume over quality. I get that. It all comes out in the end.

"Well, not all of it."

—What they don't know.

"Wouldn't interest them."

I know that Need has actually shoved Whim through the door, or in my case, up the stairwell from the car deck. Whim suggests I ignore Microsoft Word's prescription of clarity and conciseness with regards to "actually shoved" and continue on. I tell myself I need to turn that feature off, but I am lazy and do not wish to get distracted because I need to get this piece done. I feel fairly confidant the words are flowing correctly. I know there will be cutting, deletion, rearrangement, but that is for Editing, which comes later in the process.

The Process... remember—that's what it's all about. I used to think that *it's all about the process* was a lazy, caddish phrase of visual artists: an easy thing to say and in art, *nothing should be easy to say, that's what sets it apart*. A writer with whom I share a birthday says that "a writer is someone for whom writing is more difficult than it is for other people." He says this, as with most of his work, in Olympian irony. The irony, the dead pan delivery of bed pans, cigars, Russian women, horse heads full of eels, the sniggering leer of the Devil and all of them sound like some percussive symphony drumming down in the subconscious, drumming in long sentences and... but wait, the drumming comes under influence. I was speaking of process. These intrusions of influence are actually part of the process, but while always there, influences make themselves known like Dicken's Ghost of Christmas Yet to Come—in their own good time.

Time. The writer whom I quoted has a lot to say about that. Where are we? A process is nothing without time. It is the horizon of being we move towards and yet through. Like the geometric line hidden behind the Cascade Mountains, the horizon is also behind me. I am facing backwards on this boat, which suggests I should use past tense, but since I don't mind sitting backwards and this writing has the nature of a conversation that I am sharing with you, a perfect stranger on this ferry crossing, I will continue with present tense. For now. Which just was. Like the ferry, it doesn't matter which way I sit in time. I am always moving through it. But how much do I suggest to you? *When* should my words go and by that phrase, I mean: how *much* time? Do we spend it? Gods, I would love to have a wallet in my purse that could dispense money the way I spend Time. We have reached a point in time in this text where metaphor begins to intrude like the bosun's announcement over the brash PA that some idiot has left the alarm activated on their Audi or Mercedes. (It is always a German car).

I perform metaphor, which may be metaphorical itself, or not. George Lackoff will tell you that metaphor is inescapable because it's how we think. Linking like to like to like to understand because we can never really get at Kant's *ding an sich*: the thing in itself. (At this point in writing, I wonder how much German will creep into this piece—best keep it to a minimum.) Oh sure, we can *name* something but that's only the beginning of the game. In putting the pieces on the board, I can easily *call* that little castle a knight, but no one will know what I'm doing, so I reserve "knight" for the little horse's head. The names suggest a pattern of movement, of rules, but which moves I make is up to me and you, because if I break them, you won't play with me.

Enough of all that, my strategy and style has begun to become tiresome, wouldn't you agree? Partly the subject matter is to blame because I am thinking and writing (which are the same thing, really) about art. If you've read through some of my other pieces in the *Trinity* series (because the context is an anthology) you will note the theoretical, "meta" nature of this piece. Meta is a Greek word that simply means over or beyond and no, I am not going to clobber you over the head or in the gut with the bewildering world of prepositions, not to mention clichés. (Which I just did). The constituents of metaphor, translate, and carry over are more or less the same.

"Speaking of translation, what about the story of you in Japan? How did you write that?" For me, writing a story like that usually comes from an image. In that case it was a memory of a torii gate shrine on Hokkaido. Did I really see all those ghosts? Of a sort. Whether they were "actual" phantasms or not is irrelevant. I had to get to them, and the way was through the gate. Once I have the gate in my mind, I think about where to start.

Some writers write straight through, others will plot things out on index cards: both digital and paper. Like this essay, I tend to flounce around, and the beginning of "January" ("A Pearl of Loneliness" came later after I had finished it) is flouncy. That story doesn't have much of a plot. I walk through a desolate town, shuttered against the winter and strangers and then I walk on the beach at night and have a visionary experience. What the visions contained carried the import of the piece.

I wrote it on the ferries. The comfortable *Kaleetan* and the irksome *Chimacum*. *Kaleetan* means arrow in Chinook jargon and that ferry is spacious for morning commutes with lots of tables for writing. It also seemed fairly reliable at the time. Reliability is the bedrock of habit; it is the aquifer of compulsion. *Chimacum* means "you're going to miss your transfer bus on the other side." It is a newer boat, but poorly laid out, cramped and often late. It does have plenty of electric outlets, but wireless signals don't work on it very well, which I don't mind, because the Internet is the enemy of writing. Full disclosure: this piece is actually being composed on the *Hyak*, the comfortable sister-craft of the *Kaleetan*.

  The first stage of the Japan-story was simply writing. Writing memories, emotions, recollections of emotions and all of it liberated from the tedium of order and plot. And then editing. That is usually how I work; I slog through outbursts of words and then, once I am finished, I will stop and look over what I've written. I prefer to take a break in the form of a walk, which I should call a think. I subordinate a great deal, you can tell. The first piece I wrote was about how the winds would come down from Alaska, but in revision, I realized it fit better where it is. The story clocks in at 2480 words. I probably wrote 6,000.

  And here is where the Process really lifts you into the air—not in the manner of winged flight, but rather like that of a hot air balloon. I float over the words at the speed of the wind, because they haven't arranged themselves into anything coherent which is perfectly fine because this is the native mode of emotions. People will often say emotions are non-linear, but if you are one of those writers who get hung up on semantics (like me), don't worry too much about your terminology. It's not really the point of Craft if you know what the Greek word for reversal is. You may not even need one. In fact, you're not going to get any craft lectures: no pre/pro-scriptive bullshit, because this is about the writing. That's not the way to Art.

  I remember a poet once told me that I would get nowhere reading philosophy, that it was dangerous for any really good writing. Old men seemed to be full of this shit at some point, and no, I haven't found myself doing it now that I'm closer to that joker's age. Granted, he was a pretty good poet, but being full of shit and being a good poet aren't mutually exclusive states of affairs. Some may even say it's a pre-req. I suspect two things: he couldn't really get the philosophy I was reading but I was too young to sniff the ignorance through his august façade and he was making some kind of offhand remark about me fucking his colleague. Maybe he was approving? I don't know. It wouldn't surprise me the way those guys carried on about emotions and experience. I will mention briefly here that you don't need to fuck a poet to learn how to write. It can be great, don't get me wrong, especially if his dick has that curve that hits you just right so coming feels like having the inside of your skull burned out with a bubblegum blowtorch, yes and if you wonder what that is I have no idea, but they were the babbling words I could finally string together after I could speak again.

 Because the problem is, he talked about Craft a lot. The Holy Craft of Poetry and Writing. I worshipped it for a time, but I was 23 and still impressionable. He figured if it sounded good in class then it would sound even better in bed with his girlfriend who was 27 years younger than his wife. I've begrudgingly fought Craft to a stalemate over the years, and seldom believe anything coming out of a man's mouth in bed unless it's a snore. Yes, Craft is important, but it should *never* get in the way of Art. Art isn't Craft.

 Since Art can be so many things, I don't think I need to add another page on top of an already considerable mountain, but... look at the woman over there. Not that table, that one there. Yes, in the black outfit that marks her as a student of one of the cosmetology schools in Seattle. She's moved onto eye shadow now, but you missed the foundation. Dab dab dab, then buffing it in evenly. She's brushed less rouge in today over the foundation she chose, which works better with her skin tones, although to be sure, the light in here is bad. But I really admire her. She looks pretty good out in the natural light of Seattle, which, shadowless as it is and diffuse to the point of madness, is a pretty good performance. It's not easy to orchestrate that, but then again, I've never seen her wear anything but black. That sort of changes things. Can she manage her usual color palette wearing a Seahawk jersey? Can she do it with a red Prada sweater? Maybe she's capable even though her husband is cheating on her back in Silverdale. Maybe she wears that ring to keep men from bothering her. And a few women too, I suppose. I don't know much of that back story and you see where I'm going with this?

She's doing Art right now. Is it heteronormative, bourgeois, radicalizing, deconstructive? Depends how much I want to think about it, but above all it's a process. Foundation, rouge, eye liner then shadow, and finally eye lashes. She understands the context of her work, which are black clothes and a ferry with bad lighting. She also knows she'll have to do it all over again tomorrow and keep at it before she can start earning money. I'm not being metaphorical. If you want hard theory, revolution, just check out how much more work the goth chick behind her does. She came on a shapeless, blotchy-skinned 20-year-old but leaves a radiant creature of the night with black lipstick and breasts that invite you to damnation: all on the 7:20 sailing from Bremerton.

What these two women have taught me is that Craft is Important, but a vision of what you're doing is even more important. And doing it every day, which we have an ancient word for: practice. And practice takes time but give that to yourself, whatever you do. The practice becomes a habit ingrained with the desire for art, which is compulsion. I guess that is as much of a rule from me as you will get. I'm better at cautionary tales, both being one and writing them.

For many years, when I was starting out and unsure of myself as a woman, a human being and above all a writer I worried about wasting time. This was because I didn't really start writing until I was 37 or so. I had 'written' before. Even stuff I considered art, at the time. But that work scattered itself among journals and old computer disks and most of it before the Cloud ascended to the role of the Recording Angel. Yeah, there was a complete novel, I've lost it and for good reason, ultimately: it was a piece of shit. No, what changed at 37 was first, I wrote what I wanted to. But the most important lesson I learned was that I have never wasted a single moment writing. Even the cloying things I produced in high school, the lost novel, the bad poetry written in imitation of my master (hey, I got off on that at the time—I'm not going to get down on the past tense Ada for that), all of that was like each brushstroke of the women doing their makeup. It's a much bigger process than you think, and it takes an Olympian perspective to see it. Maybe that's why I've always like the Olympian Irony of that one writer. The one who said writing is harder for writers than other people.

But if I can make a suggestion, having a picture of him on your desk—he's wearing that usual look on his face, the skeptical glance that is sliding into modulated sarcasm obscuring an incandescent intellect adjudicating the fact you're filing a nail rather than writing, which is the same expression my own German grandfather used to give me and they even both came from Lübeck and may explain their mustaches and hatred of Hitler—that may not be a good idea. If you're going to be pretentious like me, then choose a writer who reminds you of someone close. This is how I let influence into the process of my writing. On my way out the door in the morning, I usually say *Guten Morgen* to my literary Grandfather. Compulsion or habit?

Oh, have I returned where I started from? No, I already did

that, sort of with the women and their makeup. My makeup is minimalist in contrast to much of my writing. I've decided that is my reaction to the woman who taught me how to really do makeup. Like writing, I didn't really hit my own stride with makeup until my 30's because that's when I dated her, and I didn't really start the writing until she dumped me. I hope this economy of romantic and aesthetic history makes more sense. I won't go into it any further because the context of the Trinity Series can help—read "The Camera Does Not Lie," from the May issue.

No, I didn't get this all written at once. It's Thursday, so I'm running a little late, but Ada got on the *Hyak* and began revising and adding a few things. Astrid eventually butted her way into the text, if not to dominate then to at least remind the writer that she is always there, just like the *other* Nobel laureate from Lübeck, Ada's presumptive Jan Bronski, drumming away in obscure lugubriation, but Ada didn't really mind. It may not make a lot of difference to the reader working through these words words words, but the process of writing them means much to her.

ABOUT THE AUTHORS

JENNIFER DIMARCO
A PNWC and Bumbershoot award-winning poet and Seattle Times bestselling novelist, Jennifer DiMarco first toured nationally as an author when she was nineteen years old. Her resume of publications includes contemporary drama, science fiction, high fantasy, and mystery novels as well as poetry collections and stage plays. For the last ten years, DiMarco has worked as a filmmaker writing and directing more than a dozen feature films, half a dozen mini series, and more than a hundred short films. She lives in the Pacific Northwest with her wife, author and actor Brianne, and their children, author and illustrator Maxwell, and producer and actor Faith. Find out more about DiMarco at www.jenniferdimarco.com.

LAUREN PATZER
Hailing from Tacoma, WA, Lauren has been an information technology guru, actor, writer and film producer among other pursuits. From the earliest days when he could sit up in a chair, he typed happily away at his grandparents IBM Selectric typewriter, writing somewhat less coherent stories than he does now. He feels the best part of writing short stories is the ability to briefly immerse yourself in a brand new world (even if it's modern day America) and tell the reader a complete, entertaining and /or thought-provoking story in just a few short pages. When he's not spending time with his wife, three daughters and grandson, Lauren is pouring over the details of his next pursuit.

HIROMI COTA

Hiromi Cota has been a special operations heavy weapons expert, an adjunct professor, a rave journalist, and the flaming-sword-swinging lead in a heavy metal opera. They (singular) have lived in nations around the world, but have settled down in Seattle with their spouse Randi and their (plural) dog Nasus. Outside of crafting queer science fiction/fantasy, Hiromi writes roleplaying games, produces the inclusive and comedic D&D radio drama podcast "Dear High Elves," programs video games, and gets into sword fights as a member of the Seattle Knights actor-combatant troupe. A reasonably complete list of their work can be found at: HiromiCota.com

AMBER RAINEY

A mom first in all things she does, Amber just happens to also be an author, actor, and award-winning filmmaker. She lives in Texas with her engineer husband, precocious son, and two cats, who vie for her lap while she writes. Amber has yet to find a medium she doesn't enjoy so she writes novels, short stories, and screenplays. Her first novel, *Eternal Willow*, can be found online at Amazon. You can visit www.amberrainey.com and www.tiny.cc/amberrainey for more about Amber and her work.

MARSHALL MILLER

After retiring as a Senior Special Agent/Federal Criminal Investigator, Marshall found a second career in writing and has a published four book series called THE TSCHAAA INFESTATION. These in-depth science fiction/speculative fiction works examine the human condition, and what people would do to survive when threatened with being eaten by an invading intelligent alien species. His thirty years of law enforcement experience and world travel provides him with the basis for the many varied characters which populate his literary works, demonstrating the good, the bad, and the ugly.

ELIZA LOEB

A United States actor, Eliza stepped in to the writing field in 2018, beginning with the Trinity Anthology for Blue Forge Press. Originally born on Guam, they had spent their life reading, writing and creating with many artistic influences. Today, Eliza channels their creativity and experiences through their writing and does their best to reach out to their readers with a subtle portrayal of empathy or compassion. Sometimes, by allowing the reader to get close to them through the pages, other times by a means of fiction. Most times with wine that rarely touches the glass. A recently published piece of Eliza Loeb's work can be found on Amazon in the horror anthology *Unnerving*. But for those of you who would like to see the human behind the writer with occasional writing tidbits, feel free to follow Eliza on Tumbler at imelizaloeb.tumblr.com.

SHEILA MENGERT

A transgender novelist, dramatist, and poet, Sheila is also a political commentator. She has a Masters Degree in English Literature from the University of Washington with an emphasis on the works of James Joyce and Virginia Woolf. Her stories in the Trinity Anthology are a debut effort for her in a new genre. Her previous books include a non-fiction book on Borderline Personality Disorder and a seven volume epic re-telling of the Sherlock Holmes Saga published under another name. The story of her transition is told in her book *Transsexualism and its Discontents: A Political Profile* available from KitsapPublishing.com under the separate editorial imprint of Trannie-Goddess Press. Sheila is currently at work on an eighth volume sequel to her Sherlock Holmes Saga dealing with The Great European War of 1914-1918 and its critical aftermath in the Peace Conference of 1919 in Paris.

CARRIE AVERY MORIARTY

Born and raised in the Pacific Northwest, Carrie still lives there with the love of her life. She raised two wonderful, if not slightly warped, children who both live close to home. When she's not yelling at her hometown sports teams on the television, she's cheering them on from the stands. She loves nature and spending time enjoying it with her family. And you don't want to attempt to beat her in any board game. They are meant to be played to the death. Find more from Carrie at www.facebook.com/AuthorCarrieAveryMoriarty/ and on Twitter or Instagram @camoriarty13.

DAVID MECKLENBURG

Much like his unseen Gemini half/fictional narrator Ada Ludenow, writer & illustrator David Mecklenburg was born in Sacramento, and moved home to Washington to attend the University of Washington. He has worked as a chef, tech support specialist, and capital project manager. You can often find him on the Washington State ferries commuting to and from Bremerton where he now lives. This story was written "on the water." For more information about David (& Ada) please visit www.hagengard.com.

ABOUT THE EDITOR

BRIANNE DIMARCO
A published short story author, poet, and writer of more than a dozen short films, Brianne has been captivated by the written word from an early age and doesn't even remember when she learned to read. She currently works as a full-time volunteer for Blue Forge Group and is the Senior Editor of their publishing division, Blue Forge Press. Brianne lives with her wife, Jennifer, and their children, Faith and Maxwell, in the Pacific Northwest. Find more from Brianne on Twitter & Instagram @indigo_bee88

Trinity is a twelve-volume series where nine radically diverse authors all create stories based on a new prompt every month. Trinity volumes are released the first half of every month in 2020 and are available wherever fine books are sold. However, you can purchase a subscription directly from Blue Forge Press and receive volumes for free.

Trinity eBook Subscription
http://tiny.cc/trinityebooks
$39.92 (plus tax) for twelve ebooks delivered to your email. You'll receive four monthly volumes for free.

Trinity Print Subscription (One Payment)
http://tiny.cc/trinityannual
$129.90 (plus tax) for twelve trade paperbacks delivered to your home monthly. You'll receive two volumes for free and receive free shipping on all volumes.

Trinity Print Subscription (Monthly Installments)
http://tiny.cc/trinitymonthly
$12.99 (plus tax) charged every month for eleven months with free shipping and the twelfth volume sent for free. Trade paperbacks will be sent to your home monthly.

Made in the USA
Monee, IL
18 July 2020